STEPHANIE TURNER

Pretty In Poison

Bethany Knox Private Investigator #2

First edition

ISBN: 9798469713081

This book was professionally typeset on Reedsy.
Find out more at reedsy.com

To Karen, for all the encouragement.

Contents

Promises, Promises   1
One Crisis at a Time   8
Thunder Struck   21
Temperature Variations   27
Burden of Proof   38
Residue   41
Worse Choices   50
Chipping Away   58
Commonplace   65
Over-Complications   73
Red Light, Green Light   84
Turbulence   90
Paula-tics   94
Peebles   100
The Point   106
Vertigo   114
Justified   121
About the Author   125
Also by Stephanie Turner   126

Promises, Promises

I sat cross-legged on my bed in the back of my white utility van and watched the monitor for movement. The motion detectors I'd set around the property were keyed to alert me to any disturbance. My van's roof top camera was set to infrared mode so I could see clearly in the dark. There hadn't been much to see so far. I'd spent the last six hours watching, waiting, and wondering if this was going to be a bust.

At least it wasn't a total loss. Most of my time had been spent crocheting a magenta sun hat by feel while I listened to Victor Powell's voice narrate his latest crime thriller. My heart was pounding, and not just because the story was thrilling - it was, but because he had called me earlier that week, requesting the honor of my company as his date - tonight! - at the annual Cormorant Cove Spring Gala. I couldn't wait.

The story ended, Victor's voice trailed away just as I bound off my final stitches, and I was about ready to pack everything in when one of my alarms went off. My heart pounded with adrenaline as I checked my display. Quadrant 4. The side of the house. That was strange. How did that one get tripped without the others being affected?

I trained my camera on the zone that had alerted me, just in time to observe a pair of raccoons ascending a drainpipe on the side of the house.

Good grief.

I had nothing better to do, so I watched them shimmy up the pipe and scamper across the gutter. I leaned forward to see them squeeze themselves through a soft-ball sized crack in the siding underneath a gable window, only to emerge about five minutes later dragging a flowing white object between them.

I trained my drone on them, following their antics as they scuttled from rooftop to tree trunk to derelict garden shed in a neighboring backyard, where it seems they had established a very soft and rather swanky nest.

The mystery of who had been breaking in and making off with my client's collection of expensive silk and satin negligees - not her creepy ex-boyfriend as she'd suspected, had been solved.

No arrests were made.

I collected my gear as the sun peeked over the horizon, chuckling to myself as my adrenaline petered out. Lilac and forsythia blooms hung heavy on their boughs, filling the air with their heady fragrance, making me even more drowsy. I considered crawling into my bed in the back of the van, stealth sleeping right where I was parked, but decided I was too close to the highway when an eighteen-wheeler roared past. I rented a peaceful residential spot in my best friend Evie's yard; I might as well get my money's worth out of it. I drove up Metro, Nova Scotia's highway system with my windows down to let the breeze blow in off the Atlantic Ocean, passed the Cormorant Cove Marina where generations of Knox's had kept their fishing boats and where I now kept my trusty kayak, and turned into the Cormorant Cove subdivision where I kept my living quarters.

I had just pulled into my parking space and snuggled into my pillows, the rear doors of my van swung wide open to let in the breeze and the fragrance of spring, magnetic mosquito netting secured into place to keep out any tiny, unwanted visitors, when a squealing seven-year-old poked through my attempted slumber.

"Aunty Bethany! I love it!"

"Happy Birthday." I smiled at Juliet. "The hat fits?"

"It's perfect!"

"Good." I said. "Now go away so I can sleep."

"But it's after breakfast. You said that's the rule."

"It has to be after *my* breakfast." I qualified; she stuck out her bottom lip. I laughed. "Let me sleep till noon, and I'll take you to the playground."

"At the beach?" She bargained.

"If it will make you go away..."

"It will if we can get ice cream, too."

"Juliet!" Evie was mortified by her offspring's manners.

"You don't ask, you don't get." Juliet quoted her mother to herself.

"You're going to get something alright." Evie promised, though she sounded suspiciously like she was trying not to laugh. "Now go play and let Aunty Bethany sleep."

"But-"

"Ice cream at the beach, french fries for lunch, and we'll have you back in plenty of time for your party." I promised; Juliet took off, pleased with this outcome. "I think you're raising a future lawyer." I told Evie.

"I think you're spoiling her rotten." Evie let the laugh out.

"You only turn seven once." I justified. "I caught the culprits."

"Culprits?" Evie caught the plural. "The boyfriend had an accomplice?"

"Wasn't the boyfriend."

"No?"

"Trash pandas."

She laughed. "Those little buggers get into everything."

"Wake me at noon?"

"Will do." She promised.

I settled myself again, and then my phone rang. I grumbled at myself for not turning off the ringer, and then answered it. "Opportunity Knox."

"I'm hoping it will answer." Nigel Essex's British accent drove all thoughts of sleep from my mind.

"Dr. Essex?" I sat up so fast I banged my head on my bookshelf. Hard.

"Are you quite alright, Miss Knox?"

"Quite." I winced and rubbed my head; a goose egg was forming already. "Thank you. What can I do for you?"

"Two things. The first; I have an employee I suspect may be selling company secrets. Gabriel Hunt has assured me you investigate such matters..."

"I do indeed."

He gave me a few particulars.

"When would you like me to start?"

"Is tomorrow morning too soon?"

"I can make that happen." I promised him. "And the second thing?"

"This evening," He cleared his throat; was he nervous? "If you are available-"

"I'll stop you there." I said, feeling disappointed. "I'm afraid my evening is spoken for."

4

"Ah, well, serves me right for waiting till the last second. Another time, then. Thank you, Miss Knox."

"You're quite welcome, Dr. Essex."

"Until tomorrow."

"I look forward to working with you again." I turned off my ringer, got an ice-pack for my head, and could not fall asleep.

I still kept my promise to Juliet. I borrowed Evie's car-seat equipped car to drive the birthday girl to the Burger & Bait Shack for fish & chips, then stopped at the Cove Creamery for chocolate mint ice cream. We ate our ice cream as we walked along the boardwalk, making our way to the beach. It wasn't much of a beach, just a strip of machine-groomed sand along the waterfront, but it seemed to fit the bill for the under ten crowd. The sun was warm, the water freezing as we dabbled our feet in the waves, the shrieks of gulls and gales of laughter from frolicking children filling the air.

"Can I play at the playground now?" Juliet asked excitedly.

"Absolutely." I assured her; she was off before the second syllable had been uttered. I laughed as I watched her work her way into a small herd of children, marveling at how easily little kids could make friends. If only we stayed that way when we grew up.

I snagged a park bench for myself where I could keep one eye on Juliet, and one on the ships sailing across the water. I poked gingerly at the lump on my head, thankful it was hidden under my mass of hair. A sound behind me caught my attention and I turned to look.

"Beth." Sam Blackwood - my former partner, stood well away from me, hands in his pockets. "I thought that was you; who else has hair that red?"

"Sam." I goggled, my heart racing. I didn't know what to say.

PRETTY IN POISON

"I thought you were in-"

"Antigonish." He nodded. "Just here for the weekend. Becca wanted to visit her mother."

I grimaced, pained for him. "Sorry."

He laughed. "I'm-"

"Sam!" Becca came storming towards him, her black eyes smoldering. "You promised-"

"I said hello, that's-"

"Too much." She snarled at him. "Go wreck someone else's marriage." She snarled at me.

Sam shrugged sheepishly, and followed her away.

I crossed my arms around my middle, feeling sick with guilt. I probably deserved that feeling. I turned back to call Juliet over, more than ready to leave, and couldn't see her.

I couldn't understand - I had only looked away for a minute - not even that long! How could she be gone so fast?

I walked towards the playground, checking swings and see-saws as I passed, poking my head under a slide hood, peeking around climbing poles. I reached the spot where I'd last sighted her. Her hat was on the ground, but she was nowhere to be seen.

I picked up her hat, my heart pounding. "Juliet?"

I climbed onto the play structure for better vantage, spinning in a circle, eyes peeled, no sign of her. "Jules? Juliet!"

"You found my hat!" Juliet scrambled up beside me.

I crushed her in a hug. "Where were you?"

"Under the slide." She wriggled free and pulled her hat on.

"Of course." I nodded, trying to sound calm, my heart rate slowing. "The most natural place in the world to be."

"Hey, aren't you a little big to be up there?" A man's voice boomed at me.

I laughed. "Hey, Marco." I managed to extricate myself from

6

the structure, wondering how I ever used to find such things fun. I turned to Juliet. "Don't go-"

"Past the gravel; I know." Juliet ran off.

"Are you here for the swings or the slide?" I asked Marco Firenze, friend from my rookie days on the police force, now the owner and operator of Paragon Security Services.

Marco laughed. "Babysitting my nephews." He nodded to the twin boys now playing with Juliet under the slide, building a sandcastle and moat from the looks of it. "All quiet on the western front?"

"Nary a peep. How is the east? Find any more secret tunnels in Cormorant Heights?"

"One was enough." He assured me.

"Keep an eye on the Essex Estate." I warned him. "He might put one in."

"Thanks for the heads up." Marco chuckled and shook his head at me. "You hurting for work?"

"I start a new job tomorrow. Why, have you got something for me to do?"

"Security audit on a warehouse property; something don't smell right. Could you zip your drone around, make me a bird's eye map of the place?"

"I'll give you a call tomorrow after I know what's up with this case," I promised. "We'll set something up."

"Deal." Marco shook on it.

This time I kept both eyes firmly fixed on Juliet as she played, and pitied any future children I might have; I was going to be an unapologetic helicopter mother. I wondered if they would look like me, or like Nigel? Good grief, Bethany. I must have hit my head harder than I thought.

One Crisis at a Time

I returned Juliet to her mother, and returned to my van for a much needed nap. When I woke, I borrowed a dress and heels from Evie, and she helped put up my hair.

"Pretty in pink." Evie squeezed my shoulder.

"Thanks to you." I squeezed her fingers.

"Thanks to good genes." She countered. "Are you nervous?"

"A little." I admitted. "I can't stop thinking about it actually. Do you think I should wear black, or navy? I want to-"

"What are you talking about?" Evie wrinkled her nose.

"The case tomorrow." I said. "What are you talking about?"

"Your date." She poked my shoulder. "Tonight?"

"Oh." I compressed my lips, my face blushing red to match my hair. "That."

"Poor Victor." Evie laughed.

The doorbell rang, freeing me from any further incriminating responses. "That's him."

"Knock him dead." Evie told me; I kissed her cheek.

Victor Powell was standing in the doorway, dapperly dressed in black tuxedo, but looking rather uncomfortable as Juliet gave him the rundown. I paused on the stairs, just out of his sight to listen.

"Are you a solicitor?" Juliet asked.

"Do you even know what that word means?" Victor demanded brusquely.

"Of course not." Juliet replied, unperturbed. "I'm only seven. Do you have children?"

"No."

"Why not?"

"Because."

"Don't you want any?"

"You ask an awful lot of questions."

"Yes." Juliet agreed. "Are you a Mormon?"

I figured that was enough, and went to his rescue. "Victor."

"Bethany," He smiled, relieved, and handed me a beautiful bouquet of pink camellias. "You look ravishing, my dear."

"Thank you." I blushed, and handed Evie the bouquet to put in water.

"What does 'ravishing' mean?" Juliet asked.

Victor was developing a slight tic under his left eye.

"It means pretty." I kissed her head. "I'll see you in the morning, little Miss Marshall."

"Have fun!" Evie waved us off from the steps.

Victor held the car door for me, and drove the not very far distance down the road to the Cormorant Cove Community Hall.

"Tell me," Victor asked as he drove. "What is the significance of Mormon solicitors?"

I laughed. "They're the only ones that come to the front door."

"I see..." He said; I wasn't sure he did.

"A local knows to come to the kitchen door. That's where everyone will be."

"Always in the kitchen? I thought women's lib solved that

years ago."

"People will always need to eat." I said. "It's human nature to gather round the grub."

"Don't say 'grub' please." Victor gave a slight shudder. "It's a vulgar term. It makes me think of slimy insects."

"Oh?" I said. "I'm sorry-"

"Not to worry." He patted my hand, then rested his hand above my knee. "You're still young enough to train properly."

That snapped my head up. "What-"

"Here we are." He announced.

I let the remark go, but felt a growing discomfort I couldn't shake.

The Community Hall was a beautiful building: granite stone trimmed in fir, the back side a wall of two-story windows overlooking the Cove. One side of the hall was filled with tables, the other side an open floor for dancing before a raised stage for the musicians. Many a formal wedding reception had been held here. As we entered I could see through to the wall of windows open to the patio, garlanded in twinkling white lights. I longed to step outside, see the ocean beyond the cove, taste the salt in the air, and feel the wind blowing through my hair. Victor seemed inclined to socialize.

He led me on his arm through the growing crowd. I felt like a decoration. And I felt out of place. I'd assumed at a spring gala there'd be bright and light colors reminiscent of spring, with women decked like flowers and butterflies. This felt like a funeral; everywhere I looked I saw black.

The exception to that became immediately apparent; one lady in pearlescent white, from the tips of her shiny white patent-leather heels to the mounds of white hair piled on her head: Edith Alderson.

I tended to avoid the news media as much as I could, but even I had picked up the name of Cormorant Cove's reigning socialite. As I recall, it was she that spearheaded the building up and re-branding of our little community, encouraging if not outright financing the local businesses; she was a bank unto herself. And also generous, donating funds to build much of the rec center, this community hall, and 're-envisioning' the community library. I wasn't sure I was grateful for that last one; I was partial to the old library, unchanged for over a century, packed wall to wall and floor to ceiling with books, as a library should be. The new modern building felt more like a cafeteria, impersonal and spare, and containing minimal books to clutter its insides. It might as well be a coffee shop.

Edith had also been the primary instigator behind the Cormorant Heights development. A lot of locals had fought the idea, loathe to give up their favorite, pristine fishing hole. But in Edith's words, 'Progress can't be stopped.' She didn't seem to let much stand in her way.

She held her own now, talking and challenging the movers and shakers of the community as they gathered around her: the fire chief, the mayor and a cadre of bureaucrats, the police chief - Patience spotted me and gave me a wink, then went back to haranguing the impromptu gathering about the recent department cutbacks. Then there were the businessmen, including Nigel Essex.

His eyes met mine at the same moment mine met his. I smiled. He smiled. And then he noticed my hand in the crook of Victor's arm. He frowned, cut his eyes away, and downed his drink in a single gulp.

Edith caught the exchange; I don't think that woman ever missed a thing. "Victor," She linked her arm through Nigel's

11

so he couldn't escape, and called us over. "Introduce me to this lovely creature."

"Edith Alderson," Victor obeyed, "Miss Bethany Knox of-"

"Opportunity Knox Private Investigators!" Edith exclaimed. "The heroine of Cormorant Heights."

"Hardly that." I demurred, embarrassed to be so singled out.

"Precisely that." Nigel insisted; I bowed my head, my cheeks burning.

"I thought I was only a nosy, interfering, busy body."

Everyone laughed politely at my joke.

"My grandmother's pearls would have been gone forever if not for you." Edith touched the strand at her throat.

"I'm glad they were returned to you." I said.

"Insurance would have replaced them, I'm sure." Victor noted.

"I don't want them replaced." Edith said. "I want these particular ones, alone."

"They are sentimental." I said.

"They are mine." Edith said simply.

"That I understand." Victor said, running his fingers up my arm.

I shuddered.

Nigel narrowed his eyes.

Victor didn't seem to notice.

Edith didn't miss a beat. "Victor, I want to have a word with you about a scheme I'm concocting."

"Oh?" Victor asked dubiously.

"A book launch, to launch my newest yacht." She explained. "Perhaps a murder mystery, based on your newest novel? We could have the Globe cover it all…"

"Oh!" Victor exclaimed. "My publicist would love that."

"Won't she just?" Edith smiled blandly. "Nigel, be a dear and twirl Miss Knox about on the dance floor while I snabble her date. That dress deserves to be shown off."

"Your wish is my command." Nigel bowed to her. "Miss Knox?" He offered me his arm, if a trifle stiffly, and led me away.

We were the first couple to take the floor. I didn't usually like to be seen – in my line of work attention was ideally avoided, but I thought tonight I could make an exception. I looked up into Nigel's eyes, and smiled. He looked down at me, and glowered.

"Victor Powell is old enough to be your father!" Nigel hissed in my ear. "You look completely ridiculous together–"

"Then don't look." I snarled, and pulled away. I tried to.

He wouldn't let me go.

"Nigel–"

"Finish the dance with me." He said tersely. "We don't want to make a scene, now."

"I never do." I noted.

He deigned not to argue.

We glided around the floor together, pointedly not looking at each other. I will give him credit; he kept perfect time, as skilled in dancing as he was in piloting his boat, and in unsettling my heart. I was supposed to be with Victor. I was trying hard to forget about Nigel. I was failing miserably at both. And just what did Nigel think he was about, anyway? What business of his was it who I went out with? What did he even care – oh... I looked up at him again. He did care.

"What is it?" He narrowed his eyes suspiciously.

"You're jealous." I smiled.

"Don't be ridiculous–"

I laughed. "I was going to go with flattered–"

"You're reading too much into-"

"Oh? Am I? I thought-"

"What the blazes is he doing here?" Nigel effectively kiboshed the discussion.

"Who?"

"Red bow-tie." He pointed with his chin. "He's the man I have concerns about." He winced. "If he sees you with me, he'll be suspicious-"

"Introduce me." I redirected. "Tell him the truth; I have a background in analysis and will be meeting with select employees to find inefficiencies and correct irregularities. He doesn't need to know any more than that."

"The truth." Nigel grinned. "What a novel concept."

"No one ever sees it coming." I assured him.

I felt Victor's gaze following me as Nigel led me from the dance floor, and cringed inwardly. I needed to make a clean break from him as soon as possible. I liked the man's writing; the man himself triggered my internal alarm system to high alert. I would rather walk home than trap myself alone with him in his car. I considered the man who now held my arm, and determined I would likely not need to walk. One crisis at a time, though.

"Harris Peebles," Nigel caught the attention of the man he wished me to investigate; the probable thief. "May I present Miss Bethany Knox..."

I studied Peebles carefully as Nigel rattled off the excuses for my upcoming intrusion into his work life; the man smiled and nodded, but I sensed he was not at all pleased. He was a short, rather obsequious little man, wringing his hands as he listened to Nigel, his smile closer to a cringe, his eyes darting furtively between Nigel and I. Maybe he had an astigmatism?

"So pleased to meet you." I held out my hand to him at the appropriate time.

Peebles barely touched it, giving me the limpest handshake I'd ever experienced. Were his hands powdered? His skin felt like a newborn baby's foot; soft, almost flaccid, not even a hint of callous to prove he'd ever done a moment's hard work.

"Charmed." He cocked his head in a facsimile of respect, but a disgusted sneer flickered across his face as he did, just for a moment, so fast it might have been imagined.

I knew what I saw, but why was it directed at me?

"Monday, then." Harris dismissed both of us – I don't think Nigel realized what he'd done, and sidled away.

My alarm bells were clanging. "Charming fellow." I said to Nigel.

"Isn't he? If he weren't such a brilliant scientist–"

"Dr. Essex?" A grating, nasal voice drew our attention. "How lovely to see you outside the work place."

"Yes... lovely." Nigel looked pained. "Miss Bethany Knox, Miss Paula McLeod, a recent addition to our HR department."

Paula waved dismissively, blushing to match her red hair as if he'd flattered her. "I only keep up morale among the staff and make sure things are running efficiently, you know, a small but important role."

Nigel smiled devilishly. "Miss Knox will be joining us on Monday,"

"Oh?" Paula looked surprised.

"She's an analysis expert; there are a few departments running not quite as efficiently as they might that I feel she can improve."

"How... lovely." Paula's tone was strained; I could feel her sizing me up. "I did not think we were supposed to wear pink with our hair color." She sniffed at my dress and patted her black skirt-set with one hand, her red hair with the other.

"Some rules were made to be broken." I said.

"Rules should always be followed." Paula stated priggishly.

"Except when breaking the rules results in such lovely consequences." Nigel contradicted her, gliding his finger down my arm, and sending my heart into a frenzy in the process. Then he smiled and waved to someone across the room. I followed his gaze to the beautiful woman - possibly supermodel, pouting at him. "I've neglected my date long enough. Till the morrow, Miss Knox, Miss McLeod."

Well, there goes my ride. "Till then."

"I would not take what he said to heart." Paula clucked after Nigel's retreating back. "He tosses away compliments the way other men toss away used tissues." She smiled in mock-sympathy at me.

"I've never heard him give you one." A perfectly lovely woman interjected herself into our conversation. She looked a little weird with her green-colored hair and multi-hued clothing, but the fun kind of weird. She shook my hand warmly; I could have hugged her; Paula bared her fangs. "Briar O'Neil, I'm one of the minions Master Essex keeps locked on the third floor; testing department."

"We try not to hold it against her." A blond man in a rather bold orange plaid suit put out his hand to me, shaking it firmly; Briar laughed at his addition; Paula grimaced. "Dean Finley, Essex's resident chemical anarchist," I laughed. "And you're Bethany Knox. I read all about you in the Globe."

"Oh?" I winced. "I didn't realize I'd been mentioned."

"Featured." Briar said; Paula ground her teeth. "Deservedly, for clearing the boss."

"We're rather protective of him." Dean added.

"I'm pleased to know he has good people watching his back." I said.

"Don't know how good we are," Briar gave Dean a wicked grin. "But we know we'd never have it so good anywhere else."

"Hear, hear!" Dean agreed enthusiastically.

"No one else would have you." Paula dripped acid.

"Oh, dry up, Paula!" Briar growled at her. "Do you always have to be such a wet blanket? Be off! Ruin someone else's party."

Paula turned up her nose with a sniff, and departed.

"Ach." Briar groaned. "With our luck she'll be at our table."

"If we beat her there we can booby-trap her chair." Dean suggested.

"Yes!" Briar agreed at once, then she turned a serious face on me. "Tell no one."

"My lips are sealed." I assured them, and laughed as they scurried away on their nefarious mission.

A bell tinkled, announcing dinner. I made my way to my assigned table where I spent a miserable evening beside Victor Powell, being alternately ignored as he loudly conversed with our table-mates, bored as he regaled me - repeatedly - with the plots of every novel he'd ever written or planned to write, and annoyed as his attentions became more physical, and increasingly invasive.

My misery was only compounded by seeing Nigel Essex at the table across from ours, smiling and laughing, sharing witty exchanges with his table-mates, receiving the rapt attention of his date, and appearing to welcome her advances. I felt ridiculous; why would he feel jealous over me when he had her? It was torture to watch. I don't know why I stayed. I'm a glutton for punishment, I guess.

I looked away from Nigel, and saw Harris Peebles. I followed his gaze; he was watching Nigel intently, studying him, copying him? The gestures he made were strangely disjointed, a crude attempt at mimicry, and making his table-mates uneasy. The ones that cared, that is; Briar and Dean appeared not to notice him, too busy with laughing behind their hands and stealing side-long glances at an uncomfortable-looking Paula, seated beside Harris; there appeared to be something horribly wrong with her seat. The rest of his table-mates were conversing quietly, laughing uneasily, obviously leaning away from him; he paid them no heed. Curious.

Victor brayed a laugh at his own joke, drawing Harris' attention. His eyes met mine, and he glared at me with a look of such intense loathing I fumbled and spilled wine all over Evie's dress. Thankfully it was white wine. It was also a good pretext to escape Victor's roving fingers, at least for a few moments. I made my way to the facilities, and dabbed up the worst of the mess I'd made of myself. I blinked back tears, pasted a smile on my face, and nearly had a heart attack when I opened the washroom door.

"Mr. Peebles?" I asked.

Harris Peebles bowed his head, his fingers clutched before him as he stood, obviously waiting for me in the hall. Nervous habit? He seemed rather anxious about something.

"Ah, Ms. Knot, was it?"

"Knox." I corrected.

"I wondered, that is, perhaps..."

"How can I help you?"

"I think perhaps I can help you..."

"I'm all ears." I smiled, trying to make him feel comfortable.

He gave that cringing smile, but then his demeanor changed. He stood up straight - I'd swear he was taller than me, his eyes grown cold, devoid of light, his voice clear and direct, taking on a hint of a British accent. "Keep your nose out of business that doesn't concern you." Peebles turned into that frail and cringing thing again, and slunk away.

I was too stunned to react, my heart pounding erratically. Did I just have a run in with Dr. Jekyll and Mr. Hyde? By the time I composed myself enough to move back to the dining area he was gone from the building. Nigel looked quizzically at me, but his date quickly recaptured his attention. Victor didn't notice. Edith certainly did. One crisis at a time...

One had been enough.

I was exhausted and drained, my mind reeling with questions about Peebles, about Nigel, about everything, and thus made the mistake of letting Victor drive me home. I stepped out of the car before he could open the door for me, and turned to face him on the doorstep.

"Victor, I'm sorry, but this isn't working-"

"Say no more, Bethany. I believe I know what you feel."

"You do?" I felt relieved.

"I feel exactly the same." He said in a way that made me certain he did not. He moved to kiss me, affirming that notion, but I turned my head. His tongue went into my ear. Ew!

"No - I'm sorry." I pushed away from him. "Just, no."

"Too soon?" Victor looked disappointed.

"Way too soon." I latched onto the idea. "I'm not ready for a relationship. My divorce was so difficult..." True, that.

"I am a patient man." He kissed my hand. "And you are well worth the," He raised his eyebrows suggestively, "Anticipa-tion."

I cringed. "Thank you for being so... understanding."

He kissed my hand, and drove off.

I stood on the steps, alone, and wanting very much to be alone. Not even Evie would be balm for my heart tonight. I just wanted to sleep and forget this nightmare of a night had ever happened.

I went to my van, punched my code into the keypad, slid open the side door, and screamed. "What are you doing!"

"You said we could talk sometime." My ex-husband sat on my bed, buck naked, defiling it with his presence.

"I said talk, Jeff, not - just - put your pants on!" I slammed the door, shaking with fury.

Evie came tearing out of the house, cast-iron skillet raised for battle. "What is it? Victor? What did he try? Let me at him!"

I burst out laughing. I sat on the steps. "Oh, Evie." I burst out crying.

Thunder Struck

Evie made me a cup of coffee. Black. Strong. Since the universe didn't seem to want me to sleep...

"How did you get into my van?" I sat at the table, back to the wall, across from a now fully-clothed Jeff.

Evie slid into the seat beside me, a further barricade against him.

"Do you mind?" He asked her.

"Not at all." She smiled, settling back with arms crossed.

"Answer the question." I ordered.

"Where were you, dressed like that?" He demanded instead, his jaw tight. "Who's Victor?"

"None of your business." Evie said.

He glared at her, then turned pleading eyes on me.

I withered. "Evie?"

She huffed and shook her head at me. "Watch yourself." She warned Jeff.

"Or you'll do what?" He scoffed.

She slung the skillet over her shoulder on her way out of the room.

"She wouldn't." Jeff swallowed. "Would she?"

I crossed my arms. "How did you get into my van?"

He turned on his puppy-dog eyes. "You look beautiful, Beth-"

"Jeff!"

"Factory preset over-ride." He sighed. "I called the van company..."

I texted my father. If I couldn't sleep... "Why are you here? Spider let you out for the evening?"

He glowered. Then his face softened. "I shouldn't have listened to him. We made sense-"

"You should have listened to him sooner." I put down my phone. "We never made sense."

"We could have."

"If the world was different, and we were different people." I shook my head. "We tried. It didn't work."

"We could try again..." He offered his hand. "What would it hurt?"

"My dignity and self respect." I dug my nails into my elbows lest I be tempted. "Not to mention my rib-cage, and my-"

He winced and pulled his hand back, balling it into a fist. "I said I was sorry about that."

"You said that every time." I reminded him. "But nothing ever changed."

Lights flashed through the window as a car pulled into the driveway. Dad already? Evie must have called him before I texted.

"This time will be different." He promised; I started to shake again. "I went to counseling. I got help. I still love you, Beth."

"I love you, too."

He smiled.

"But I don't trust you."

His face turned into a thundercloud.

22

Marco strode through the door, ready to hurl lightning. "He touch you?"

I shook my head no.

"I forgot I can't trust you either." Jeff spat at me.

"You were warned to stay away from her." Marco snarled at him.

"You can have her." Jeff snarled back. "I don't need damaged goods."

I turned my head away, feeling struck.

Marco let him pass, and slammed the door behind him. "Jerk face."

I laughed. "Jerk face?"

"Nephews." He grinned. "You OK?"

I nodded my head yes, then shook it no, then rested it in my hands, elbows on the table. "I don't know what to do."

"Park behind my place, it makes you feel better?" Marco offered.

"After I finish electrifying the lock pad." Dad put in as he came through the door. "Did he hurt you?"

I jumped up to hug him. "No." I felt the bulge of his holster under his jacket, and hugged him tighter. "You can do that? Electrify the pad?"

"I'm sure going to try." He kissed my forehead. "Marco. Thank you."

"Anytime, Boss." Marco nodded.

"I want in on this!" Evie demanded, barreling into Dad.

He laughed and hugged her too.

"I got to get to sleep," Evie announced. "Working double-shifts tomorrow. But there's rhubarb pie on the counter; you all stay as long as you want." She kissed my cheek. "Anything you need..."

"Thank you." I hugged her tight. "I'm good now."

Evie headed upstairs. Marco headed for the pie. Dad kept his arm around me till the shaking subsided.

"I'm never going to sleep." I rubbed my eyes with the back of my hand.

"You up for a fly-by?" Marco asked.

I felt Dad tense, about to protest on my behalf.

"I've got energy to burn; I might as well do something useful with it." I said.

Dad pursed his lips, then nodded. "I'll reset your locks."

Marco finished inhaling his pie. "Let's not waste any time, then."

I hopped in the van to change, feeling nervous and exposed, turning at every sound. Why were there so many sounds at night? I had to stop myself from opening every drawer, checking to make sure everything was in place, see that nothing was missing. There'd be time for that later. I grabbed my drone, my bag, and my metal construction clipboard; that thing comes in handy. I wanted something in my hands firm and solid to cling to, and hold in front of me for protection. It fit the bill.

Marco drove us out to the Newell Lake Industrial Park. There was a good mix of warehouses, offices, and labs, as well as restaurants, casino, and a swanky hotel on the water that I'd visited before while following a target. I looked out and tilted my head back to see the top of the Essex Pharmaceuticals building where I was slated to go tomorrow, though I guess later this morning would be more accurate.

Marco rolled through the checkpoint after a word with his men to make sure all was well; all was.

"What is this place?" I asked.

"Part of Alderson Holdings."

"As in Edith Alderson?"

"Assume so." He shrugged. "I'm just a lackey hired by a third party; don't get to sully the upper crust, you know."

"Their loss; you're a diamond in the rough."

He laughed. "This should do."

I stepped out into the cool night. The wind was blowing, but not enough to disrupt my drone. Not yet. I closed my eyes and tilted my head back, inhaling the promise of rain to come. I set my laptop on the trunk of the car, synced up my infrared camera, and set my drone free to fly.

I followed the perimeter fencing all around the property, and especially along the water. "That's an awfully big ship for a lake, is this–"

"Connected to the seaboard via canal-locks." Marco supplied.

"That's right." I remembered now. "The kerfuffle over this development was drowned out by the one at Cormorant Heights."

"Almost seemed planned."

"You believe in coincidence now?"

"Not for a second." Marco said. "Keep fishing." He nodded at my controls.

I got back to work. "Anything in particular you want to see?"

"Don't know." He shrugged. "Can't name it, and maybe it's nothing; I just know something's not jiving with me. Don't want my name associated with the place if they're not above snuff, you know?"

"I know." I said, in full agreement with his sentiments. Some jobs were more trouble than they were worth, especially if the trouble landed on you. I went back and forth in a grid over the warehouses and the lots surrounding the buildings, then recalled my drone. "I think that's all she wrote. Unless you want me to poke inside?"

"I don't want to push it. Not yet, anyway. I'm contracted for the gate and perimeters only; no internal checks, no shipment arrival checks, and absolutely no outgoing vehicle checks."

"That's a little..."

"Not jiving." Marco nodded sagely. "Pay was too good to pass up, but the longer I'm here..."

"I hear you." I yawned. "I'll mesh these up tonight."

"Take you home now?"

I considered that. A rumble of thunder in the distance decided me. "Is your couch vacant?"

"For as long as you want it."

"Thanks, Marco."

Temperature Variations

I slept like the dead on Marco's couch, waking a little past dawn when he started breakfast. He dropped me back at my van on his way to work. I felt nervous and fluttery as I entered the new key-code Dad had set up, and had to stop halfway through to borrow Evie's skillet before I could complete the procedure. I held my breath, not wanting to make a sound. I opened the door, listened carefully, and then put in my head. I exhaled. I survived, and made myself go in the rest of the way. I turned on every light, checked every surface, every drawer, every nook and cranny. Nothing seemed out of place, but everything felt off somehow. I felt off. I knew Dad ran a bug sweep, but I ran another. I felt secure enough to shut the van door. I ran another. I showered. I ran another.

I didn't try to eat. I wrapped myself in black, then made myself change into brown slacks with cream blouse and green cardigan. Professional, with a bit of color. Something a calm, rational, reasonable person would wear. Something I could run in. I felt fake.

I drove myself out to the Essex Pharmaceuticals building, and parked in the visitor lot before the entrance. Nigel Essex stood just inside the doors, waiting for me. I picked up my bag of gear, debating on the contractor clipboard, rejecting it, then grabbing it at the last second. It was a strange sort of security blanket. We all have our quirks.

I walked towards the entrance doors of the massive glass and steel building, and stopped, frowning at the security pad mounted outside. I crooked my finger, and Nigel came through the doors to meet me.

"Miss Knox?" He was blunt and direct, almost terse, as usual.

I followed his lead easily, feeling far cooler towards him now than I had the night before. "Dr. Essex." I tapped the Castellan Keypad mounted by his door. "If I'm analyzing your security, I may as well start here."

"Is there a problem?"

I pulled out my key ring, selected the key I wanted, and unlocked the cover. I held up the key. "I bought this for $8.99 on-line; this single key will open every single Castellan product manufactured in North America."

"Oh my word."

"I can flick this." I flipped a latch, and the front door unlocked. "And voila - I'm in. And while I have this open," I reached into my bag and pulled out my cloner, swiping it over the card reader mounted inside the Keypad cover. "I now have the access numbers from every card that's ever been swiped through your system. $59.99, same place I bought the key."

Nigel looked ready to spit nails.

I figured I was earning my keep.

"I'll have to replace everything!"

"Not necessarily." I closed the cover. "Once you know and address the vulnerabilities, the system does work well. I'll make recommendations in my report for correcting the known issues, or I can suggest replacement systems if you prefer?"

"I'll look at both options, please, and then decide."

"Very good."

I frowned at the front doors – plate glass with no frame – you might as well not bother locking them at all, and made a note to find replacements. Then I looked up, taking in what I assumed to be the cutting edge design of the structure before me, all the edges being cut off and canted at different angles, a true marvel of geometry. I couldn't decide if I liked it or not, but it was certainly interesting.

"The windows are angled for maximum solar exposure, and for its opposite." Nigel explained as he opened the door for me, noting my gaze. "We're working on a topically applied solar absorbent film that will be highly effective even on minimally exposed windows, several actually, that look to be promising for mass residential use. If we can get the murkiness worked out." He frowned at a particularly foggy pane.

"Good for new builds?" I asked.

"Good for everyone." He led me past an empty reception desk with no security guard anywhere that I could see – that earned another note, and towards a bank of elevators. "Affordable for everyone. That's my key stipulation. Well, that and it has to actually work."

"A minor detail." I laughed; he chuckled. "I never considered solar residential films as the prerogative of a pharmaceutical company."

"I like to play." Nigel smiled, and gestured to me to proceed into the elevator. He selected the third floor. "And I encourage it in my employees; we never know what product will take off until it does. If they have an idea for a passion project with even a glimmer of promise, then I'm happy to fund the research, and if warranted, supply the opportunity to bring it to market."

"And split the proceeds."

"So cynical, Miss Knox?" He tsked. "I invest in my employees, at times a great deal, but not only that: I front all the risk. It's only fair that I receive a share of the profits in return."

"I can't fault your logic; that does seem quite reasonable."

"You needn't look so pained to admit it." He teased.

I laughed, warming to him again. Good grief, Bethany.

The elevator doors opened, and Nigel gestured me ahead. The hallway here was as empty as the main floor lobby had been. Our footsteps echoed as we walked.

"Is there no one else here?"

"Not likely. We had a busy week - end of quarter deadlines are always insane, so most everyone was glad for the weekend. There's always a few die-hards on the fourth floor that live to work; if they want to spend their time that way, I'm happy to let them. I think at least one of them sleeps on the couch more often than not. The cleaners run through on weekday evenings. We should have this floor to ourselves."

"What can you tell me about Peebles?" I asked. "What's concerned you?"

"He's always been a little... different." Nigel said. "That's almost part and parcel around here though. All my best scientists are a trifle mad, but the harmless variety; they talk to themselves, wear mismatched shoes, wander off mid-conversation when they have an idea. I take them as they are, and they put out their best effort for me."

"Harris Peebles though..." I gently pulled him back onto task.

"He does excellent work, but it feels like he's holding back. He's always kept to himself, and the others have respected that and held back from him in turn. But recently, he's changed.

Drastically. He's become extra furtive and secretive, and now the others give him a wide berth in the hall. I'm not sure it's entirely conscious on their part."

"What else has changed?"

"He's always been punctual to the point I'd say fastidious, but he's begun arriving late and leaving at odd times, and lately, there's an edge of spite to him that I've never noticed before. I strongly sense something is off, but he hasn't chosen to confide in me. I'm at a loss."

"What's been stolen?"

"Information. Possibly."

"Possibly?"

He waved his hand. "I'm probably making a mountain out of a molehill; there's likely a perfectly reasonable explanation. You must think me a fool-"

"No, quite the opposite." I assured him. "It's better to trust your gut and be wrong than ignore it and find out the hard way you were right. The times I've ignored my intuition I've come to regret it. Don't second guess yourself. If you're wrong, you won't have hurt anything. If you're right, it's always better to know the truth-"

"Is it?" He stopped walking, looking at me intently.

"What's best isn't always what's comfortable."

He bowed his head. "If I made you uncomfortable last night-"

"It's fine, I-"

"I had no right to speak to you the way I did about Victor. It's none of my concern-"

"Let's just focus on the task at hand, shall we?" I said stiffly, my face burning. With anger, or with disappointment? Did I want him to be concerned? I determined not to think about it.

"Please." He nodded tersely, leading me on again through

31

the maze of corridors.

"Information has possibly been stolen?" I led.

He supplied. "Raw data that could potentially be used to reverse engineer my formulas and methods. The processes for each of the individual components are separate, kept deliberately at arms length-"

"That can't engender much trust-"

"Needs must." Nigel said. "I've worked very hard to build this little empire. I've put in countless hours and sleepless nights trying to make it work. And it has worked. I won't give up the fruits of my labor for nothing; the government takes enough in taxes already. No, the parts must be kept apart until the end. Peebles is the final step, where all of the separate moving parts come together. He's made himself the lynch pin in my operations; without him it all falls apart."

"But now you think he's deliberately pulling it apart? Selling to someone?"

"I pay him enough he shouldn't feel the need. I'd pay him more if he wanted, but he seemed content - no - he seemed quite pleased with his last raise. I don't understand the change I've seen in him. He's grown so smug and evasive. It's completely out of character from the man I've employed for the last eight years. The changes in him made me suspicious, and that made me look into the work coming out of his department-"

"You have access to all the data?"

"Every transmission within my company."

"All? Outgoing e-mails?"

"Legally." He said defensively. "If it's within my systems, I can see it. As a point of personal ethics I do not look at my employees correspondence, not unless I've been given serious reason to do so."

"And Harris Peebles behavior changes are reason enough?"

"He's evaded my direct questions about my product's development. I did not feel a choice-"

"And it's perfectly within your ground as his employer to know every aspect of your business." I agreed, trying to stem the defensiveness.

He nodded, mollified that I wasn't assigning him blame.

"There's clear evidence of theft?" I asked.

"There is clear evidence of attempts, or what I can only assume are attempts to decrypt and send files of aggregate data. It came from Peebles lab, and given his behavior-"

"It is concerning." I agreed.

"It could be benign." Nigel frowned. "A system error - we've had enough of those. I don't want to accuse Peebles unless I'm certain it's him deliberately trying to bypass my security protocols. After what I just went through, being accused of Clark's murder... I will not accuse anyone without absolute proof on my side."

"I understand." I said. "I think it's wise."

"Thank you." That lifted a weight off his shoulders.

"When did you notice the changes? Recently, you said..."

"Within the last month."

"Before Clark Bevan's murder?"

His jaw clenched. "Yes." He said tersely.

"I'm sorry to have brought it up again-"

"No. I could see how... It should be considered. Others have certainly changed toward me since then."

"Has he?" I wondered. "Has it increased?"

He closed his eyes, thinking. "I should say so. Peebles' appearance at the Spring Gala - I've never known him to socialize before."

"Furtive and secretive, and socializing?"

Nigel shrugged helplessly. "I can't figure him out. He's always avoided company gatherings like the plague. He sits apart in the cafeteria, hiding behind a stack of papers or books. They make an effective barrier around him, and he seemed content so I've granted him his space. These changes in him are weird."

"What else has changed then? What's triggered him to change?"

"That's why you're here." Nigel grinned. "Help me figure it out, help me see the pattern I'm too close to see."

I considered. "Did Harris Peebles have a passion project?"

He frowned at that question, and then grunted. That was out of character for him, a crack in his ever present reserve.

I looked at him carefully. "Yes? No?"

"No. He came to me with an idea, and I rejected it."

"Why?"

"It was inappropriate. Outside the mandate of my company's ethical policy, and well outside my comfort zone."

"Does his request fit the time frame for his behavior change?"

"It does." His jaw tightened. "Blast it. I should have seen that connection. If I hadn't been so consumed by Clark's death-" He shook his head. "I apologize, Miss Knox. I may have just wasted your time."

"Or you may not." I countered. "A disgruntled employee can wreak a lot of damage."

"I can't believe he'd be capable-"

"Could you have believed Charlie Bevan capable of killing her husband before you heard her admit it?" I cringed at the effects my words had on him. "I'm so sorry. That was utterly insensitive-"

34

"That was true." He said stiffly. "And entirely appropriate. Think nothing more of it."

I bowed my head, knowing I'd be thinking a lot more of it, and kicking myself for saying it. Hard. "I think you're right to be concerned by Peebles."

"How so?" Nigel pulled out his key fob, swiping the door in front of him. Nothing happened. He tried twice more. "Strange."

"Can you open any door?"

"It should open every door." He said irritably, and I thought a touch embarrassed that it was not cooperating now. He tried the door across the hall, then two more; they all opened.

I tried my cloning device; it worked everywhere I tried, except on Peebles door.

"You see my concern now?" Nigel asked. "He's up to something in there."

Did I detect a note of vindication? I stood on tiptoes to look through the glass window high in the door. "He's dead in there."

"What?" Nigel demanded, pushing in front of me to see.

I pointed to the far corner of the room, and the abnormally pale face of the man lying on the floor, eyes open, unblinking, his body concealed behind his desk. "That is him?"

Nigel shook his head yes. He leaned his back against the door, then sank to the floor, his head in his hands.

I called the police, then texted my father and Gabriel Hunt - our lawyer, in that order.

"Why does this keep happening?" Nigel asked. "Am I cursed, or are you?"

"It's me." I assured him. "Red hair attracts bad luck."

He laughed sardonically. "Blast it. Poor Harris."

I looked through the window again, trying to determine what

had happened to the man. He blinked. "He's alive!" I jiggled the handle of Peebles' door again.

Nigel tried his fob again, then fumbled for his phone. "I'll have to call security-"

"Are there request to exit sensors?"

"Sorry?"

I tapped his fob. "You need a badge to get in the room; do you need it to get out?"

"No, just to enter-"

I dug in my bag, pulled out my bottle of keyboard cleaner, and stuck the straw in the nozzle. I threaded the straw through the gap at the top of the door and sprayed until I heard a click; the door unlocked.

Nigel ground his teeth. "How?"

"It's a passive thermal sensor; any sudden temperature variation trips it," I held up my bottle. "I just lowered the temperature."

"You'll put this-"

"In my report." I pushed the door open, and nearly fell over. Powerful fumes from some chemical I couldn't identify assailed me, assaulting my senses.

Nigel pushed past me to get to the window, and the door banged shut behind him.

I turned to open the door; the handle was missing.

Nigel pounded on the window, and couldn't budge it.

I ran at it with my metal clipboard. It made only a tiny star shaped scratch. I hefted it again but tilted hard to port, the fumes getting the better of me.

Nigel took the clipboard from me. His first swing cracked the glass. His second shattered it. Cool, fresh, fume-free air flooded into the room. Nigel leaned his head out, and took a deep, gulping breath. He looked to me, then grabbed Harris under his arms, dragging him towards the window; I helped Nigel prop him up, holding him between us before the window.

"Miss Knox?" Nigel said weakly over top of Peebles' head.

"Yes?"

"Remind me to put you on retainer."

I laughed. And then I blacked out.

Burden of Proof

"Bethany?" My name came from far away. I felt someone shake my shoulder, then caress the back of their fingers across my cheek. "Beth, wake up."

I opened my eyes. I regretted calling the police. Greatly. "Jeff?"

"Do you know what she inhaled?" He asked someone over my head.

"I have a broad idea." Nigel responded; he sounded extra irritable. Worried? "I'll need to run some tests to be certain."

I tilted my head to look at him, the movement leaving me extra confused and disoriented. Nigel was holding his head, a gray blanket over his shoulders, the ceiling a duller gray behind him. Or was it the sky? Were those clouds?

"Peebles?" I asked.

"An ambulance took him; another's on its way for you." Jeff assured me, smoothing his hand over my hair.

"I'm fine." I pushed his hand away, or at least made an effort; my hands flailed limply, uncooperative. Traitors.

"You're not fine, baby." Jeff contradicted. "But you know I'll take care of you." He bent his head to kiss me.

Nigel looked away.

"No." I lurched, trying to get away, and spilled myself onto concrete. Outside. I tried to sit up, to crawl, but I couldn't make my limbs respond properly. I started to cry.

"Darling, come." Nigel helped me to my feet, holding me to keep me upright.

"I've got her." Jeff snarled.

"I don't think she wants you." Nigel said.

"I made that clear last night." I made it abundantly clear now, if I hadn't before. I forced my will, found my feet, and pushed free of Nigel. "We're done, Jeff."

"We're done when I say we're-"

Nigel stepped in front of me. "It's poor manners to contradict a lady; I will not tolerate-"

"Stop!" I stepped between them. I bowed my head, making myself smaller, non-threatening. "Just, thank you for your help." I said to Jeff. "I do appreciate it."

He huffed, but he took the dismissal for what it was - an excuse to get a hold of himself, and walked away. Was that proof he'd gotten help? He was trying...

I turned to Nigel. "Thank you, Dr. Essex."

He took a rather hard seat on the edge of a planter, bowing his head to me. "You're quite welcome, Miss Knox."

"You're quite shaky." I noted, shaking myself as I sat beside him. "What did we inhale?"

"Something that should not have been within my building." Nigel frowned at the doors.

"Mr. Peebles rejected project?" I surmised. "Could he have been working on it anyway, tacitly, without your approval?"

"I think perhaps..." His eyebrows furrowed.

"What is it?"

"Harris wasn't one to make a mistake." He said. "If that had been his formula, the one he brought to me, we would not have survived."

I considered the room we had been in; the malfunctioning card-entry, the missing door handle, the sealed windows... "I don't think he was supposed to have survived."

Nigel nodded agreement, then held his head, pained from the movement. "I have a state of the art air filtration system running throughout the laboratories; it's designed to come on and vent the room if the gaseous profile alters beyond a certain threshold. That it didn't come on..."

"Someone tried to kill Harris Peebles, and nearly took us with him."

"In my labs." Nigel was furious.

I looked across the quad towards Jeff. "Perhaps I should call Officer Dover back?"

"After we took such pains to drive him off?" Nigel looked at me askance. "No, my original stipulation is still in effect; I will not accuse anyone without absolute proof. Will you help me find that proof, Miss Knox?"

I considered only briefly. "Gladly, Dr. Essex." A thought occurred to me; I sat bolt upright.

"What is it?" Nigel asked.

"Air filters aren't working; would all the labs be affect-"

"Oh my word." Nigel shot to his feet. "Officer Dover!" He ran for the door, Jeff and his partner on his heels.

I stood to follow, and then wobbled to my knees on the concrete, hoping no one else had been inside.

Residue

I heard shots fired - bullets taking out glass, and started to sob uncontrollably. Sirens came closer. I pulled myself together and hauled myself to the keypad. I opened it with my skeleton key, and let the paramedics into the building. I slumped to the ground beside the door, waiting I don't know how long for the stretcher to come back through. I knew it would. I knew who it would be carrying. I just knew.

Jeff came out first, and put his arm around me. "I thought so..." He gave me a squeeze. "You let yourself feel too much; this is why you were never a good cop."

I slipped out of his grip, perching on the planter edge again. "It's why I was never a good cop's wife."

He shrugged. "What angle are you taking?"

"How do you know I'm taking an angle?"

He just looked at me.

I withered. Then I sat up straighter, squinting at him. "You're letting me-"

"Use the strengths you have," He quoted my father; my hackles rose. "You're good at ferreting things out, I'm good at pounding down doors. This needs ferreting-"

"If you think this will get us back-"

"This is direct from Chief Patience." Jeff smiled, pleased to have upset me. "We're down to four men, including a sergeant, per shift,"

I winced at that - at minimum it should have been twelve officers and a sergeant, a baker's dozen; the last round of budget cutbacks were more like amputations. No wonder Patience had been so upset at the Gala.

"We don't have the boots on the ground, but since I told her you were here..." He kissed my cheek before I could stop him. "You've got an hour before forensics arrives and I have to chase you out, so get up there with your camera. We're still on the same team." He walked away before I could explode on him. He knew me too well; he knew I wanted in more than I wanted a fight.

I hated when he was right. I grabbed my camera bag from my van. My legs still felt weak, but the longer I was up, the less shaky I felt. I inhaled deeply. There didn't seem to be any lingering effects from whatever gases I'd breathed in upstairs. I went back up to the third floor.

I stepped off the elevator. Dan 'Spider' Webb, Jeff's partner, saw me, and turned his back to look out the window, ignoring me. I was good with that. Then I was suspicious. It wasn't like him not to make a dig at me. I pulled out my phone, dialing Patience as I made my way to the labs.

"Dover?"

"Knox." I corrected; I still needed to change my phone display. "Did you really give me the go ahead, Chief?"

"What are you talking about?"

"That's what I thought." I sighed. "I'm at Essex Labs-"
She swore.

"Did you speak with Jeff or Webb?"

"Spider's pulling strings again." She tsked.

"At least I know who to blame." I said. "Since I'm here; I don't want to step on any toes, but I was hired by Essex to look into a matter that may prove related to the current mess-"

"You don't think it's accidental then?"

"Circumstances tell me otherwise." I said. "You weren't going to send in forensics?"

"And I wasn't going to pass Spider over for promotion again. You want to let him know?"

"I wouldn't deprive you of the pleasure."

She laughed. "Smart girl. Stay out of it. If the union weren't tying my hands you know I'd have him out of it. Don't repeat that."

"Sorry, must have lost connection. Didn't hear that last bit."

"Convenient." She laughed. "Thank you."

"Permission to poke around?"

"You're not under my jurisdiction anymore."

"Professional courtesy."

"Appreciated. Go to town, just-"

"Touch nothing, be gone when the white suits get here."

"Like I said, smart girl."

"I'll be in touch." I hung up, and dropped my bag. I had my white coverall suit in the front pouch. I pulled it on, and tucked my hair under the hood. First rule to avoiding a hassle: look like you belong. It also kept me from contaminating a crime scene; bonus points. I walked past the paramedics stuck in the hall till the medical examiner arrived and relieved them, and went up to the rookie stationed on the door.

"You got here fast." Rookie said.

"In the area." I said. "I'm just taking preliminary pics; rest of the team will be here shortly."

He nodded and let me pass without further ado. I scanned the lab quickly. It looked like a lab. I couldn't name half the equipment or what it did; Nigel would have to fill me in on what was relevant. I wondered where he was, then focused on the task at hand. I took pics of it all, working counter-clockwise around the room, getting a feel for the place, trying to build up a sense of what was normal before I encountered what was most definitely not normally here.

Things were kept neat, carefully ordered and labeled, doors and drawers kept locked when not in use. Except for the cupboard with the key hanging from the lock. I used my pen to carefully pull open the cupboard, taking pictures of the bottles and their labels inside. Most of the names were 37-syllables long, names I hadn't encountered since high school chemistry and had mostly forgotten, and if I'm being honest, gladly forgotten. Acids and bases and virulent neurotoxins? Not my thing. I closed the cupboard door.

The windows along the back wall had been shot out, letting in fresh air from the lake. The fumes were still strong enough to give me a headache, still strong enough to let me know this room was their source; Harris Peebles lab next door had likely filled with toxic fumes either as an accident or as an oversight. Or as a cover?

It wasn't unheard of, the guilty party dosing themselves with a small amount of poison to make themselves look innocent, and to throw off the scent. For a man that behaved furtively, evasively, secretively... Nigel claimed Peebles would never make a mistake, but maybe the dose had been stronger than intended?

I came to the last row. I braced myself. I could sense the wrongness around the other side of the lab desk. I knew what

I would see: Briar O'Neil in her colorful hair, her face pale and still. I knew. I was never ready to see it. I made myself look anyway.

It wasn't her.

Dean Finley lay on the ground, dressed in comfortable jeans, black t-shirt, and white lab coat. He might have been down for a nap except for his eyes open, staring at the ceiling, his cheeks too pink, his lips cherry red.

I stood still. Stunned. Him? How? Why? I was so sure...

My mind wheeled and clanked as my camera whirred and clicked. Dean, not Briar. Where had that assumption come from? What had triggered it? What was wrong with this picture? Why had I formed it? Why him, and not her?

More questions, no answers. I took more pictures. My head spun. The fumes were stronger here, the fresh air from the blasted out windows barely able to compensate. The longer I was there, the dizzier I became.

Dean had been sitting on a stool, looking at a slide under a microscope. I took a shot of what he'd seen; I peered into the lens, careful not to bump it, not even to breathe on it. It looked like algae. Biology, not chemistry? Was this Dean's passion project? I photographed the body; his finger tips were streaked with blue. Ink from a pen? From something else? Where was it? What was it?

I spun around, looking for something out of place, looking for the source of the fumes, and couldn't see it. I walked towards the inner wall, the one shared with Peebles' lab, complete with shared metal grate, and could smell it. I walked closer; I could see it. Tiny green flecks splattered the floor and walls around the vent. I knew. It was in the vent, inside the air filtration system, whatever it was. I heard a clicking noise, blew out my breath, and ran from the room, slamming the door behind me before the vent started spewing in earnest again.

"Hey!" Rookie hollered.

I pressed my fist to my pounding temple. "You need a breathing mask on if you're going to be here long." I told him, and wished I had one. I probably shouldn't have gone in there without one. Hindsight is a wonderful thing when it works. "Keep the door shut, keep the vapors in the room."

He paled, and crossed to the far side of the hall. "What killed the guy? We couldn't tell-"

"Whatever it is, it's in the vents." I said.

"There you are, Miss Knox." Nigel came up behind me, also dressed in white coveralls. He handed me a breathing apparatus. "Shall we examine the scene next door?" He pointed the way to Peebles' lab.

"Am I supposed to watch that, too?" The rookie asked nervously.

"You're fine as you are." Nigel assured him; he definitely knew where he belonged, and had no problem playing the man in charge. Nigel pulled on his breathing mask, and I followed suit. "This should work now." He swiped his fob over the entrance plate; sure enough the light turned green, and the door to Harris Peebles' personal lab opened.

"How?" I asked.

"I can over-ride entry-card protocols from my office. That was at least one feature I had the foresight to install. Why I didn't think to put in tamper alarms-"

"You know the poison's in the vent system?"

"I figured that out when we found Finley." His voice was like granite, the veneer of stone I knew he wore when he was most upset.

46

"Do you know what it is?"

He held up a fistful of vials. "I intend to find out."

"Do you have security camera footage-"

I could hear him grind his teeth through his mask. "Footage for the entire building for the past 24 hours has been corrupted; there's nothing but static and squelching. I've reset the system; I saw you putting on your suit and figured I should do the same." He tapped his mask proudly, then shook his head irritably. "Someone's covered all their bases."

"Someone thinks they have." I said. "There are always clues, little bits of behavioral residue - things we do so often, so unthinkingly, that we don't even notice them. We always leave a trace."

"Let's find it then." Nigel set right to work, pulling out swabs to go with his vials, testing the air vent and various surfaces around the room for any residue of the substance that killed Finley and incapacitated Peebles.

I pulled out my camera, and started taking shots of Peebles' office. His lab was smaller than the one next door, a space for an individual, not a team. I was surprised he hadn't fatally succumbed to the gas in here; it must have filled this small space faster than the room next door. Maybe he hadn't been in here long enough to be affected?

I stepped carefully around the broken glass, eyeing my clipboard and laptop bag with longing. I knew better than to remove them before forensics had done their thing.

None of Peebles' cupboards were locked; if it was just him working in here and the lab door was kept locked, I supposed there was no reason they should be. He trusted they were safe. Bottles and vials were meticulously labeled, precisely arrayed, alphabetically ordered. I opened his top desk drawer, also unlocked. The pens and pencils were evenly arranged, spaced to within a millimeter's error margin. Obsessive order from an anxious and insecure man; part and parcel. What I would expect. What I didn't expect was the bookcase.

Five shelves were perfectly ordered, the subjects largely chemical treatises and references, books with their spines in perfect parallel to one another, precisely perpendicular to the edge of the shelf; that was in keeping with the rest of the space. One shelf stood out; books had been shoved in at random, sideways, backwards, upside down, spines bent and mangled as if they'd been hurled in anger, one looked as if someone had tried to tear it in two. Cracks in the composure? These were more like canyons, and completely out of place in this tightly ordered little room.

I took several pictures, then selected the topmost book: 'How to Fix Your Broken Self and Become the Person You Should Have Been' by one Dr. Oaron. I flipped open the cover and read the dedication: To Harry, Love Paula. Interesting... All the other titles on this shelf bore similar treatment - variations on a theme of not just mere self-improvement, but self-renovation, even self-re-creation, and all bore the same inscription from Paula. Why had Peebles kept them? They'd obviously upset him. I piled the books back as I'd found them, and tried to recall any interactions between Peebles and Paula the night before at the gala. I found I could not. They sat next to each other, but I never saw them speak or even exchange glances. Of course, he was busy with his strange Nigel impression, and she was busy trying to find a comfortable sitting position. Were they deliberately ignoring one another?

"What can you say about Paula McLeod?" I asked Nigel.

"Nothing good." He quipped. "That woman drives me up the

wall."

"I take it you didn't hire her?"

"It was a board decision; one that makes me long for the days when I was sole dictator. Some feel my encouragement of employee creativity damages the bottom line too much; Miss McLeod was their attempt to reign me in, or perhaps to punish me? It's torturous having her peek over my shoulder all the time."

"Did Peebles feel the same? Briar O'Neil and Dean Finley certainly had."

"I–" He tilted his head, considering, but got distracted. "This is locked." Nigel said, jiggling the door to a supply closet.

"Curious." I said.

"How so?"

"Peebles keeps vials of neurotoxins and potent acids side by side in unlocked cupboards all around the room; what would he have to protect in there?"

"I'm dying to find out what kind of residue he's left behind." Nigel looked slightly discomfited by what had just come out of his mouth, then gave a helpless shrug and tapped the lock. "Any more tricks in your arsenal?"

"A few." I pulled out my key ring, found the little wire hook I kept there, and used it to trip the latch. The door swung open. "Oh my."

"Well," Nigel's eyes widened. "That was unexpected."

Worse Choices

I stood looking at a rather impressive collection of photographs, newspaper clippings, and what must have been glossy advertising images, all carefully trimmed and arranged on a large poster-board taking up almost the entirety of the closet, and all featuring Nigel Essex.

"Should I be flattered or terrified?" Nigel asked. "What is this?"

The board was so full my gaze wasn't sure where to land, but finally it settled; emblazoned across the top was a title: Become Who You Should Have Been. "It's a vision board."

"A what?"

I tapped the title. "Dr. Oaron's merchandise to match his books. The vision board is a visual goals board. From the little I've heard of the man, he encourages his victims to pick a focus – a person they want to be, and alter every aspect of their lives to become that person-"

"His victims?" Nigel laughed at my word choice.

"It fits." I shrugged. "He's proscribing a delusional fantasy to insecure and vulnerable people instead of encouraging them to make the best of the reality they're given. I can't pretend to like his methods, or his results." I frowned at the poster. "Harris Peebles wants to be you."

"I suppose there are worse choices." Nigel furrowed his forehead. "But all these personality changes; is that really how he thinks I behave?"

"It would explain his attempt at a British accent."

"Oh my word." Nigel rubbed his temple, or he would have if his mask hadn't been in the way. "Shall we burn it?"

I considered. "It would be best if Peebles chose to do that for himself."

"People rarely choose as you want them to." Nigel noted. "Unless you have a stellar marketing team to influence them."

"Maybe your marketing team could do something with this?" I pointed at the poster before us.

He grimaced at me, and started to close the door. "We'll just pretend it doesn't exist."

I stopped the door with my fingers. "If a thorough search is conducted, I doubt we'll be able to pretend."

"They wouldn't put it out there? What about confidentiality-"

"One pic from a phone, posted on-line... It's not supposed to happen, but it does." I shimmied the board out, feeling only slightly guilty as I did. My protective instincts were stronger. Maybe Jeff was right and I hadn't been that good of a cop? "I think you've had enough awkward publicity this past month."

Nigel grunted like he'd been kicked. "I strongly agree."

I picked up the board. And then I stopped. My conscience kicked in. "Darn it." I looked at him, torn.

"What is it?"

"Removing evidence..."

"Leave it." He said instantly.

"But-"

"That's Peebles' twisted mind; it's nothing to do with me."
That granite voice told me what he really felt. "And besides, we
don't want you to get in trouble."

"That's unavoidable." I pulled out my phone, dialing Patience
again.

"What did you do?" She demanded.

"It's what I'm going to do." I sent her a picture of the board.
"If Spider sees it-"

"Don't let him." She blew out a breath. "Copies of your
pictures, and your report before end of day."

"You'll have it." I promised. "Thank you, Chief."

"You owe me." She hung up.

I was afraid of that.

Nigel's relieved grin made it worthwhile. "How do you
propose we get it past the hall monitor?"

"Window." I pointed. "Third floor, right?" Nigel nodded, but
my question was rhetorical, confirming to myself. I dug in my
sack of goodies and found the cordage I wanted; it should be just
long enough. I slipped the poster board into a black garbage bag,
also from my sack, tied the cord to the bag, made sure the coast
was clear, and lowered it to the ground. I let go of the cord, then
I put my head out farther, looking towards Alderson Holdings
and their security cameras pointing back towards me. I pulled
out my phone.

Marco answered. "You gotta change your display."

"Remind me later."

"You gotta cold?"

"Gas mask - I'll explain later. I'm at Essex labs; do the security
cameras at Alderson Holdings cover their lot?"

"We've got a clear shot of the front doors and their loading bay."

"Continuous coverage?" I crossed my fingers.

"24-seven."

"A gallon of extra sauce if you can pull me the last three days."

"You're on." Marco said. "I'm off at noon."

"Donairs are at one." I promised, and hung up.

"Good news?" Nigel asked.

"Potentially." I smiled, hope growing. "We've got a lot to analyze today, so we better disappear before the real forensics team appears." I moved to open the door, and stopped. "Darn it."

"What now?"

"No handle." I examined the latch; this side had a secure plate cover so my hook wouldn't reach. I checked the hinges; they were not going to pop with the tools I had on me. We were stuck. I pulled out my phone.

"Calling the door?" Nigel asked.

"Calling someone just outside."

Jeff answered. "You kept my name."

I cringed. "The phone company hasn't changed the display; don't read too much into it-"

"No - it's a sign, babe. The universe wants us back together."

I wished I'd called my father. "The universe has bigger things to worry about-"

"Then why are you calling me?" His tone was teasing, playful, hopeful; darn it. "I know what you-"

"I called because I'm trapped in a lab on the third floor; I understand you're skilled at pounding down doors..."

"I am... But we haven't talked like this in a long time. Maybe we should wait-"

"Did I mention I'm locked in a very small room, with Dr.

Essex?"

"I'll be right there."

"Thank you." I hung up.

"Was he the only alternative?" Nigel's voice had taken a chilly turn.

"I'm sure there were worse choices." Just as I'm sure my face was turning the same color as my hair. "Although I struggle to think what they are right now."

I couldn't tell whether the smile he gave me was sympathetic or sardonic.

I could tell from Jeff's expression when he opened the door what he was thinking.

"Thanks for the assist." I said stiffly, holding out my hand for a handshake, and nothing more.

"That's all I get?" Jeff got a lung full of fumes from the room, and started to cough.

"Sorry." I said, not feeling very sorry at all. I felt worried. I should not have called him. "That's all I can give you." I left him swearing in the hall.

Nigel and I doffed our gear, and I texted Patience to warn forensics to bring their bio-hazard gear, and extras for the team on duty.

"Donairs at one, was it?" Nigel asked.

I laughed. "With extra sauce." I promised.

Nigel went to his private lab upstairs to test his samples; I went downstairs and outside to recover Peebles' poster-board shrine of Nigel.

Spider was standing on top of it. "You tampering with evidence, Scarlet?"

I cringed at the nickname; I'd hoped it wouldn't stick. "You know me better than that."

He didn't buy it, and flashed me his biggest grin. "Wonder what Patience would say, if she knew you were poking around a crime scene?"

"Her exact words were 'go to town'."

That wiped away his grin. "You talked to her?"

"Professional courtesy." I kept my face carefully neutral, biting the inside of my cheek to hide the grin trying to form; I could win against Spider, as long as he didn't think I was getting too much over him. "We keep in touch; actually I have her on speed dial. Want me to call her so you can verify?" That was probably pushing it.

He scowled and pushed off from the wall, grinding the board under his heel before he stalked away.

I sighed in relief, and carried the board back to my van. The space didn't feel threatening anymore, but it didn't feel like home anymore. I turned on my rooftop cam so no one could sneak up on me. I coiled up the cord and tucked it back in my bag, then peeled down the plastic bag to make sure Spider hadn't caused too much damage. The largest picture, right in the middle, had a wrinkle I was able to smooth with my fingers, and a heel shaped divot I couldn't pry up with my finger nails. I flipped the board over to see if I could press it up from behind. I yelped, jumping back in shock, my heart pounding.

If the side with Nigel's images showed what Peebles wanted to be, then this showed what? All that he despised? All that he wanted removed from his life? The images were disturbing. All women – all red heads – eyes and mouths defaced so only gaping holes remained, bodies torn and mangled. The images were pasted on haphazardly, sideways, upside down. Like the books on his bookshelf, the ones from Paula McLeod...

I tried to detach myself, tried to think objectively, but it was hard to separate myself from the images I saw; it was hard not to identify with so many women that looked so much like me. Maybe Jeff was right; I cared too much. It wasn't about me.

What did Harris Peebles see?

I looked closer. The women were all fully clothed; this was violent, but it wasn't sexual. It was personal. It was retaliation. This lashing out was an attempt to desensitize and distance himself, to control something over which he had no control, no power, no voice. He felt helpless. Anger, pain, fear. He took out the eyes and the mouths; things that saw into him, things that judged him and found him wanting, things that told him how pitiful he was. Had they pushed him too far? Had he rigged the air filtration system trying to make them stop? Why target the lab then? Why not Paula's office? Why Dean? Why wasn't it clear to me?

I flipped the board over so I wouldn't have to look anymore. Now all I could see was Nigel. Peebles could have chosen worse. I struggled to think of any who were better...

I watched through my camera feed as the forensics team finally arrived on scene and entered the building. Jeff stood at the entrance, watching my van. Bile rose up inside of me. I tried to blame the vapors, whatever poison it was I'd inhaled, but I knew it wasn't that.

I should not have called him.

I shifted the board aside and reached for my laptop. "Darn it."

It was upstairs in Peebles' lab. I looked at my camera display screen; Jeff was outside the door now, standing in the quad, his gaze still locked on my van.

I texted my sister, Hailey: REMOTE WIPE LAPTOP.

There was nothing on it anyway. I kept it clean.

I froze. I forgot how to breathe. I gasped, gulping in air.

I pushed the tabletop aside, ripped the cushions off the bench seat and slammed up the storage lid. 2-1-3, not 1-2-3. My backups were out of order. Had he copied them, tampered with them, or just moved them to mess with me? I slumped to the ground, hyperventilating.

I looked at the screen. Jeff sat on a planter, his arms crossed, watching my van, smiling.

"I hate you!" I screamed at the screen.

I needed to move. My legs shook so much I could hardly stand. I threw up in the sink. I wobbled like I was drunk to the cab. I felt gross. Defiled. Carrying a thousand pounds of weight on my back. There was no escape from it. No escape from him.

I should never have called him.

Chipping Away

I tore out of the lot, driving aimlessly, rushing nowhere, just trying to get away. My eyes blurred between blinks. My heart hurt with every beat. I kept moving. I pulled in at Deadman's Island. I turned off the engine, stepped out the door, and threw up in a tangle of hawthorn.

I wobbled to the water and rinsed my mouth. The salt tasted better. The cold numbed my fingers. I held my hands under till they matched my insides. I splashed water on my face, then sat on a boulder until my breathing came and went in time with the waves. I was as calm inside as I was ever going to get. I needed to move. Focus on something else...

It felt like time to divide, and hopefully conquer; I texted the four names to my sister to hunt down their social media profiles, then I texted the names to Nigel to see if he could pull their employee records, and then I texted the phone company to change my name on my phone display.

I pulled out a blank notebook, and started writing down everything I knew about Harris Peebles, Paula McLeod, Dean Finley, and just to round things out, Briar O'Neil. It wasn't much, but it was a place to start, and my gut was telling me the answers were here. What were the questions: who killed Dean Finley, and why. Nigel's thief would have to wait. Was Nigel's thief the killer? I wrote that thought down, examining it. I couldn't rule it out.

I frowned at the page, and specifically, at Briar O'Neil's name on it. How did she fit? Did she fit? I didn't know why, but I was loathe to take her off my list. I circled her name. What had I seen or heard last night that was making her jump out at me now? Why was I surprised to see Dean and not her lying dead in the lab? I ran through the previous evening at the Gala in my head, scribbling out a rough transcript of everything I remembered, every sight, every gesture, every word spoken. Nothing leaped out. I didn't feel any closer to an answer. What was I missing?

I decided I'd done about as much here as I could. I pulled up my anchor, and drove off in search of answers.

When chipping away at a problem, a lot of people recommend going after the smallest bits first, working methodically, whittling away until you're left with one clean piece to tackle. That never worked for me. I had inherited a large portion of logical and analytical thinking from my father, but I'd also gotten a healthy dose of raw emotional instinct from my mother; whatever bothered me the most, that was what I tackled first. Just now, Briar O'Neil bothered me more than anything.

I got her address from Nigel, and headed up Cormorant Cove Road to see if she was at home. I wanted to speak to her in person. Her address was at the Cove View condo complex, a corner unit, right on the water. Nigel must have paid his employees very well indeed. Jeff and I had looked there once, and walked away; our combined income just wasn't enough. He hadn't been happy. He blamed me... I shuddered, and pushed away that memory.

I parked in the driveway beside a mint green convertible with fuzzy, rainbow-colored dice hanging from the mirror; that had to belong to Briar. I walked up the short flight of steps and rang her doorbell, watching the sailboats on the water as I waited.

"Miss Knox?" Briar looked confused to see me.

My attempted smile came out as a grimace. "Miss O'Neil," I bowed my head. "Could we have a word?"

"I don't think I like the sound of your voice..."

"I have bad news." I didn't believe in beating around the bush. "Dean Finley is dead."

She took a sharp breath in, and blew a shuddering breath out. "Come in." She led me up the stairs to her living room, directing me to a couch. She pressed herself into the corner of the love seat directly across from me, tucking her feet up underneath herself, wrapping her arms around her middle protectively, trying to keep out the hurt. "What happened?"

"It's still being investigated. There was some kind of gas leaking out of the air filtration system; Dr. Essex is analyzing it-"

"An accident?" Her voice hitched.

"Maybe."

"You don't think so." She was sharp.

"I have serious concerns..."

"How can I help?" She asked. "Dean was my friend." She swallowed hard. "I want to help."

"Just friends?" I dove right in. "You seemed quite close last night."

"We tried; it didn't work." She shrugged. "Some things just aren't meant to be, you know?"

"I know very well." I nodded, understanding perfectly. "What can you tell me about your work environment? There seemed to be some animosity between you and-"

"Paula McLeod." Briar sneered.

"Why?"

"You met her."

I nodded. "I'd like your take on her."

Briar blew out another shuddery breath. "I don't think anyone likes her. She rubs everyone wrong."

"How does she do that?"

"Existing?" She gave a bitter laugh. "She was supposed to be increasing efficiency, but her 'mid-morning-meetings' disrupt our most productive time. They were supposed to be ten minutes max, but they usually stretch on closer to an hour, all her, all her rules – droning on and on, telling us everything that's wrong with the way we're working, with our attitudes, with our appearance." She tugged a strand of her green hair for emphasis. "'You are the representative of this company, and your appearance must reflect...'" She copied Paula's nasal whine, and shuddered. "It's sheer torture."

"You're not the first person I've heard use that description." I said with sympathy; she didn't seem surprised. "Dean seemed to share your feelings."

She smiled at some memory. "He was leading the charge to get rid of her."

"Get rid?"

"Fired, not–" She shuddered again. "Dean liked to play pranks on people, but he wasn't usually malicious. She almost inspired him to change."

"How did Harris Peebles react to her?"

She grunted like she'd been kicked. "Odd ducks flock to-gether."

"They were... um, flocking?"

She laughed, but it was a bitter sound, full of hurt; grief

61

catching up to her. "I'm pretty sure... He was her pet project, but he was so far out of her league she must have had vertigo looking up at him. He could have had any woman; I don't know what he saw in her."

I frowned at that. Cringing, obsequious Harris Peebles didn't seem at all appealing to me; I didn't get what she saw in him. Nigel said he was brilliant, but I couldn't see how that would make up for his personality, or his mannerisms, or his demeanor, or any other aspect of him. Must be a scientist thing? Nigel did say they were all mad...

"The only way the rest of us got any relief was if he was there to distract Paula's attention. I almost feel bad for encouraging it."

"How did you do that?"

"Little things." She shrugged. "Hints and suggestions to Paula, ways she might... encourage Harris to improve. Like I said; it got rid of her."

"What did it do to him?"

Her lips disappeared – compressed into a thin line, her eyes cut to the side; a guilty expression if ever I saw one. "I'm not sure it was appreciated."

"I'm quite sure it wasn't."

Briar hung her head. "You don't think he hurt Dean?"

"He was hurt himself; he's in the hospital, and we're not sure if he's going to wake up."

"Oh," She mumbled something indecipherable, burying her head in her hands.

"I'm very sorry." I said. "That was a lot to drop on you. Maybe another time–"

"No." She lifted her head, and scrubbed at her eyes, trying her best to keep her emotions under tight control. "You're here now. What else do you want to know?"

Where did I take this? I had planned out reams of questions, mapped out different directions to guide her, but here in the moment they all felt like they would lead in circles. I let my gut lead. "Passion projects. Do you know what Dean was working on in the lab? It looked like some kind of algae..."

She shrugged. Lying, or insecurity, or did she really not know? "Dean had something new going every week. A bit ADD, you know? Half the people at work are on some kind of spectrum. I stopped getting interested in his work long ago; it never stuck."

"Did Harris Peebles-"

"If he had anything going on, he didn't share it with me." She shrugged; she did it so often I decided it must be a nervous gesture. "He kept to himself." That confirmed what Nigel had said.

"Did Paula have a project?"

"Besides Harris?" She shrugged. "Who knows?"

"What about you?" I asked.

"I've been spending all my creative energy trying to thwart Paula." She gave a guilty smile. "Not a very efficient use of my time..." She slumped a little, winding in, closing herself off, grief taking hold.

"Do you have someone-"

"My mom's supposed to come," She checked her watch. "Anytime now." She gave me a weak smile, her eyes watery. "Thanks."

I left her to herself. I stopped my van a little way up the street to write down my notes and impressions. What had I learned? Not much. Again. I felt frustrated, like I was missing something that should have been obvious. I didn't know what it was because I still didn't know what I was looking for, or where

63

to look for it. You don't know what you don't know until you know; all you can do is chip away...

A woman I assumed was her mother pulled into Briar's driveway, and I pulled away from the curb. I stopped at Paula McLeod's apartment complex, but there was no answer at her door, and none on her phone. I left her a message, then drummed my fingers on the steering wheel, trying to decide what to do next. An incoming phone call solved that problem for me; I answered, and turned my wheels to Cormorant Heights to meet with Edith Alderson.

Commonplace

I hadn't been out to Cormorant Heights for a few weeks, not since the day Charlie Bevan was arrested for her husband's murder. It made me uneasy. I wondered how Nigel could stand it, having his home as the backdrop for that scene? At least he could leave it. I carried my home around with me, a turtle hauling its shell... It was supposed to make me feel free, but now it was weighing me down, making me feel vulnerable. I pushed those thoughts away.

Cormorant Heights had changed. There were more leaves on the trees, more flowers in bloom, more construction complete; an actual gate was installed on the security entrance. This time I was stopped and questioned, and my ID checked and recorded before I was allowed to drive in. Marco's handiwork; I was glad to see it.

I drove down Cormorant Heights Drive and around Cormorant Landing Road, almost all the way to the end of the canal. My heart fluttered to see Nigel Essex's estate across the mouth of the canal; I don't know why. The scaffolding on his starter castle had come down, the stone work complete, and work had begun on his boat house. I lost sight of it as I turned onto the Alderson

Estate driveway, wondering what Edith wanted with me, that curiosity driving thoughts of Nigel away. Mostly.

If Nigel's place were a starter castle, here before me was the real deal. It looked like a heavy stone medieval fortress, minus moat and portcullis. I had to wonder; was Edith the damsel, or the dragon?

I couldn't help smiling as I tugged on the bell pull; that was a nice touch. The arched oak doors swung inward to admit me, and I was led by a butler - though maybe castellan would be more apropos, through to the very modern formal living room. I was disappointed.

Edith stood to receive me. Even in these modern surrounds I felt the urge to curtsy and address her as Lady Alderson. She looked exactly as I imagined snobbish upper-crust royalty should appear; meticulously coiffed, expensively dressed in white from head to toe again, frowning with an air of utter disdain that I would dare to sully her carpets with my commonplace presence. But then a warm and lavish smile burst forth, breaking through my illusions.

"Mrs Alderson-"

"Edith, please." She took my hands in hers, and led me to a seat beside her on the couch. "I'm so happy you could come." She sat comfortably, her ankles crossed primly before her, hands clasped loosely on her lap, no doubt trained during the same era as my grandmother that to be ladylike was to sit that way.

"I'm happy to be here. You have a beautiful home." I copied her pose but without the hand clasp, and copied the warm smile she presented to me - genuinely. Edith's personality was magnetic, and I couldn't help liking her.

"You must be curious as to why I asked you here today." She

began.

"I confess I am."

"And I must confess, though I think you know, that I quite deliberately tried to send you away with Nigel Essex at the Spring Gala."

I felt the blood rise to my cheeks at the memory of dancing with him. "And not just for a chance to speak with Victor alone." I stated. "That much I perceived, although the why escapes me..."

"I knew you were intelligent." She nodded to herself; pleased she was correct? "The 'why' is because I am a nosy, interfering, busybody-"

I laughed.

"And I am concerned."

"For me?" A virtual stranger she'd just met; I thought not. I shook my head. "For whom?" I corrected.

She smiled, and lifted a picture off the table beside her. "For her." She tapped the woman in the photo; the supermodel-like beauty Nigel had escorted to the Gala. My heart stuttered and contracted painfully, thinking of them together. "My niece, Celia Vanderly."

I swallowed, hearing her name; the Vanderly's were synonymous with money and power, controlling or influencing almost every industry and institution in this hemisphere. She wasn't just a supermodel; she was a supermodel with superpowers, and I felt even more ridiculous than I had the night before. "I recognize her, but I do not know her."

"I wouldn't have expected it." Edith said. "I would think you move in quite different circles."

"Quite." My smile felt a little stiffer; there was a class disparity here, and I had just had my nose rubbed in it. "What precisely do-"

"I meant no offense." Edith briefly pressed my knee with her fingers; she at least wanted to appear sincere. "Celia's world has been deliberately limited. There is a downside to our... privileged way of living. It can be at times confining."

"I imagine safety would be a paramount concern." I offered. Did she want Celia protected?

"Quite." She smiled, glad we could share some common understanding on our very unequal ground. "I shall come to the point. Celia is my only brother's only daughter, and I love her dearly, but I do not love her for Nigel Essex. They are a horrible match; all that they have in common is looks and money, and contrary to popular belief, that is not enough to build a life upon."

"And you want me to..."

"I would like to hire you to investigate how best to drive them apart, and then do it."

My hackles rose, furious on Nigel's behalf. I hated seeing him with someone else, but I hated more the thought of him being manipulated. "Shouldn't that be their choice?"

"If you could step in and prevent a train wreck before it happened, wouldn't you?"

"Why do you think-"

"I *know* because Celia is incapable of thinking. She's inherited her mother's beauty and a considerable portion of her father's wealth, but neither one of them spared a brain cell or even an ounce of common sense for the poor girl. Nigel appreciates her beauty and would gain incredible contacts through an alliance with her, but little else. When the novelty wears off, she will be cast aside and ignored or replaced. I do not want her used that way. I don't want her to be hurt."

"She's an adult-"

"She's a nitwit, but I love her, and while I respect Nigel's business acumen I do not trust his brain is in full control of this situation. Rather, I fear it is purely his brain and not his heart involved. What man's ever is?"

I bristled. "Nigel Essex does nothing without careful appeal to logic and reasoning, as well as having a deep concern for the people around him. He has a great deal of heart invested in everything he does. You're selling him short."

She leaned back, her eyes widening in surprise, smiling like the cat who caught the canary. "You're in love with him."

I compressed my lips. Hard. I opened my mouth to argue but no sound came out.

"Say nothing." She held up her hand. "I see I've played my hand poorly." She tapped her fingers against her lips, emphasizing that self-satisfied, almost smug expression covering her face. "I do like when forces conspire to work in my favor without my having to pay for them."

"So we're all pawns in your game-"

"Oh, darling, don't be hurt." She laughed and pressed my knee again; I shifted away from her touch, preparing to bolt. "I'm merely one of the players, and I'm very much on your team."

"As long as you're getting what you want." I qualified.

She nodded, not disagreeing. "It could also get you what you want..." I glared at her; she did not seem at all perturbed. "I'm too self-aware to be selfless, but my intentions are not entirely selfish." She leaned back, perfectly comfortable in herself despite having caused me discomfort. "I'm old. I won't live forever. I want all of my family to be as happy and as comfortable as possible, and I have no qualms about stepping

69

in to make the way smooth for them."

I leaned away, regarding her, analyzing her. "I think I understand your motivations, though I'm not comfortable with your methods."

She laughed. "My methods are merely a means to an end. Age has given me experience, if not always wisdom, and my experience tells me this pairing is wrong and must be discontinued. I will do whatever I need to do - within reason, of course - to ensure the safety and future harmony of my family members. Surely that is not a wrong desire?"

My heart thudded strangely. What's reasonable for one person didn't always hold for another. "I can't fault your desire."

"Good." She smiled, pleased, leaning forward to tap my knee again. "Good. Now if there's nothing further, I will not take up anymore-"

"There is something further." I broke in before she could dismiss me.

"Oh?" She leaned back, cool and calculating, perfectly reserved, not showing any emotion until she decided if it were worth her while.

What I wouldn't give to have her self-control. "Alderson Holdings; your shipyard and warehouses on Newell Lake-"

"What of them?"

I decided blunt honesty was best. "I don't know precisely." I admitted; she frowned. "But the security protocols you've enacted there seem strangely disjointed, and in my mind inadequate to protect your interests."

"From the goodness of your heart?" Her smile was frosty. "Sometimes it's best if the right hand doesn't know what the left hand is doing."

"But a house divided will not stand." I countered.

"You know your bible."

"I went to Sunday School. I was taught right from wrong. Something at your property feels wrong to me."

She examined me, cool and detached. "There is nothing precisely illegal–"

"Precisely?"

She smiled and nodded; awarding me a point? "Perhaps it might appear a bit underhanded to those that know no better. Lake going vessels do not have the same tariffs and duty applied as ocean going vessels. Nor are they inconvenienced with the same level of scrutiny. I can ship and receive my goods for far less this way, and keep more of my earnings in my pocket and out of the hands of politicians–"

"And the people they represent–"

"I can employ more people at a higher wage than they'd earn otherwise, keeping them and their families off the government dole, and instead, paying income taxes to the government. This way the government gets plenty, so do the people, and so do I. It's win-win, and according to the rules of law written by our government, it's also legal. As I said, I have no qualms–"

"I do."

Edith narrowed her eyes, ready to lambaste me.

"Not for your shipping arrangements, however."

She set her mouth, and then nodded, allowing me to continue.

"Security isn't checking shipments in or out, nor permitted even to enter the warehouses to check them. It's unusual in an operation that size to not insure careful and thorough oversight. The right hand doesn't always know what the left hand is doing... Do you monitor the operations yourself?"

She tilted her head, examining me again, cool and detached.

71

I bowed my head. "Forgive me if I've overstepped myself-"

Her smile bloomed and she squeezed my hand; I felt relieved. "I've allowed my nephew to run the shipyards, preparing him to take them over. Perhaps I shall look into the matter. I'm old, but I'm not out of the game just yet. Thank you for your concern."

"Thank you for listening."

She patted my hand. "Things have a way of working out far better than we can hope or imagine."

"Aristotle?"

"Oh, I like you." She squeezed my hand again. "You just might have the makings of a worthy adversary." She laughed.

I laughed too, but nervously. I couldn't tell if she was joking or not.

I was banished from her presence in any case, guided through her home and shown out the door by her castellan. I wasn't sure what to think of her. I wasn't sure what I felt. Shock and awe?

The road to hell is paved with good intentions... I couldn't fault Edith for intending the best for her family, but I detested that arrogance, that belief that she had the right to control anyone else's life that way. Using every tool in your arsenal to reveal the truth was one thing; manipulating others to manufacture the truth you wanted was another. Lifestyles of the rich... That wasn't fair. Money is just a tool; it's how you choose to wield it that matters. It's how you choose.

Over-Complications

I chose to call Paula McLeod again; still no answer. I didn't bother to leave a message this time. I tried Nigel; same deal. I drove up the Cove roads, went round the roundabout, up Quinpool, and turned into the office lot. I pulled into my spot beside Dad's, grabbed the backup drives from my storage compartment, and pulled the poster board from the back of my van to take in with me. Fresh eyes might see something I missed. That's what I hoped. Hope splattered on the floor when I walked in the door.

Dad looked terrible, his face was drawn and haggard. "Your new locks work?"

"Very well." I hugged him tight. "Thank you."

"No more run ins?"

"Well..."

"Bethany."

"Jeff was first on scene at the lab."

Dad started to pace.

"He behaved. Mostly. I need to wipe my drives. They were out of order-"

"I checked them last night." Dad said. "They weren't touched till I touched them."

"Oh." I slumped in relief.

Dad tensed even more. "What did that man do to you?"

I couldn't look him in the eye.

Dad pulled two chairs out, turning them to face one another. He took one, and pointed to the other. "Sit."

I held up my bag. Deflecting. Avoiding. "I need to run these-"

"Bethany."

I knew better than to argue with that tone. It rankled a bit; I was a grown woman, yet here I was, hopping like a child to obey. Old habits die hard.

Dad took my hands in his.

This was serious.

"I haven't asked you. I haven't pushed you. I've given you your space and your privacy because I knew you'd tell me when you were ready. But when I receive panicked messages from Evie and then from you at one o'clock in the morning-"

"I'm sorry-"

"I'm not. I am your father. You were right to call me-"

"I probably over-reacted."

"You probably didn't react soon enough." His eyes flared with anger. "I've never asked you... I think I was afraid to hear the answer." I started to shake. "Did Jeffrey hurt you? Did he hit you? Is that the real reason for your divorce-"

I couldn't meet his eyes. I started to cry.

"Damn it, Bethany-"

"You don't swear!"

"And damn Jeff!" He swore again. "And damn Sam-"

"Sam didn't know-"

"He was your partner - of course he knew! He was supposed to have your back - not take advantage of a vulnerable woman

74

and then scurry off like a coward with his tail between his legs when his actions caught up with him!"

"I wasn't innocent-"

"I know you. You were afraid, reacting in fear, reaching out to someone you trusted who was supposed to keep you safe." He argued; I couldn't refute him.

I tried anyway. "I knew what I was doing. I could have stopped it, and I didn't. It's not Sam's-"

"I'm glad you're taking responsibility for your actions, but you need to stop making yourself a martyr for his."

My head snapped up.

"You did not sin in isolation; you shouldn't suffer alone."

I crossed my arms tight around my middle.

"My little girl was hurting, and I saw it, and I looked away. That makes me as much of a coward as Sam Blackwood-"

"Daddy-"

He hugged me tight. "I failed you, my girl, and I'm sorry. I won't look away again."

I deflected; his hurt was hurting me too much. "Please don't tell Mom."

"Beth, your mother-"

"Will explode. She thinks it's uncomfortable at church now; it'll be worse when she unleashes thermonuclear war-"

Dad laughed. "Explosions can be cathartic." He brushed his thumb over my cheek. "You shouldn't be the only one carrying the blame for this disaster."

"I'm not. Sam's exiled himself; he's punishing himself. Jeff's been punished enough-"

"He deserves to be-"

"He knows it, and he knows now he'll never get me back. But he's trying to get help-"

"You're making excuses-"

I spoke over him. "A public crucifixion will not do anything to heal him. Please, don't tell Mom."

Dad pursed his lips, watching me; I looked away. "I'm glad to hear you say that; that he won't get you back."

"You're deflecting."

"Am I?"

"Dad."

"I will not tell your mother. But Ray is going to hear-"

"Dad!"

"The truth needs to out. Ray, or your mother?"

I was furious. I knew he wouldn't compromise. I chose the path of least resistance, the path of most deflection, and picked my brother-in-law. "Ray."

"Your mother's going to be hurt when she hears it second hand-"

"I'm sorry." I knew Dad would bear the brunt of it when Mom found out; she'd explode on him for not telling her, but this way, not all of creation would feel her wrath. He could take it. The way gossip traveled in these parts, it would happen all too soon.

"You can make it up to me by coming to Sunday dinner tomorrow."

I laughed bitterly, and shook my head no. "Maybe next year."

He laughed, and kissed my forehead. He knew when not to push. He tapped the bag with the poster board. "What do we have here?"

"A picture's worth a thousand words; see for yourself."

He opened the bag, looked over the images of Nigel Essex, and pursed his lips. "I think we can find you a better outlet for your-"

I smacked his shoulder. "This is Harris Peebles' handiwork.

Not mine."

Dad blew out a breath. "I can't tell you how relieved I am."

"You haven't seen the other side yet."

He flipped it over. "Oh my."

I could tell he felt as disturbed as I had when I first saw it. "What do you know about Dr. Oaron?"

"That quack on all the talk shows?"

I laughed. "That's him alright." I turned the board back to Nigel's images. "This is one of his eggs, and I think it's become something of Peebles' obsession."

"Become what you should have been..." Dad read off the title, and pursed his lips again.

"Oaron recommends that his clients pick a person they want to be, and work hard not just to become *like* them, but to become them. They are supposed to actually remake themselves in their chosen one's image."

"Never wish for someone else's life," Dad shook his head. "The grass is always greenest on top of the septic field."

"Peebles seems to have latched onto Nigel's worst qualities in his attempts to emulate him."

"Power-hungry domination?"

"That's not fair!" I leapt to Nigel's defense so fast I had vertigo. Was Edith Alderson right? Was I in love with him? I refused to entertain the thought. "I've never seen that in him."

Dad raised an eyebrow. "What have you seen?"

"Anti-social evasion." I flipped the board. "There's a fairly noxious red-head at work singling out Peebles as her pet project, and providing him with the means of his own deconstruction."

"What cruel intentions–"

"I'm not sure she sees it that way." I frowned. "My first encounter with her... She's so arrogant that she might honestly believe she's helping others."

Dad frowned at the board of mangled red-heads. "The road to hell is paved with good intentions."

"Peebles is in a living hell, a nightmare he can't escape."

"Was this a suicide attempt?"

"I don't know. I honestly hadn't considered..." I did now, and was second guessing everything I thought I knew. Was the entry-pad disabled so no one could get in to stop him? The handle removed so he couldn't change his mind? The window sealed for the same reason? I had thought Harris Peebles might have been an unintended victim and Dean Finley the target; maybe I'd had it backwards? "It's a possibility. It feels off though. It doesn't sit right."

"A suicide never should sit right." Dad patted my arm sympathetically. "It's easy to over-complicate the truth."

What was the truth? I had no answer to that. Not yet. It was time to look for one. Where was I supposed to look next, though? I wasn't sure, but sometimes looking in a completely different place will give you an idea. But sometimes, it's just a good way to deflect. I tried not to over-think it.

I stepped to Dad's computer, downloaded the images from my drone, and began the task of layering them to make a seamless map for Marco, wondering all the while.

"What do you think?" I asked Dad as I printed the map.

"I think we're in trouble." Marco said as he entered.

"What's happened?" Dad demanded, instantly on high alert.

Marco grinned. "I'm hungry, and I don't smell food."

"Brat." Dad shook his head at him.

Marco's grin grew. He handed me a disk with the security footage from Alderson Holdings I'd asked for.

"Thank you." I said to Marco. "Where's Hailey?" I asked Dad.

"I'm here." She answered for herself as she came through the door. "I had a few errands to..." She trailed off as she saw the poster board; the Nigel side. "Um, Beth, we need to find you-"

"It's not mine!" I insisted.

Marco laughed.

"Good." She said. "Cause between that and your picture in the Globe, you had me worried."

"What picture?" Dad asked before I could.

Hailey set down the donairs she was carrying, and held up today's copy of the Globe. The front page held a full-color, heart-shaped picture of me dancing with Nigel under the heading 'Love Blooms at the Spring Gala.'

"Oh, good grief." I rubbed my temples.

"I wonder what Harris Peebles would think of that?" Dad smirked at me.

I gave him a flat look.

"Not a bad shot." Nigel took in the picture as he came in the door. "You do look lovely in pink."

My face turned pink.

Marco laughed.

Nigel grinned, and handed me a data stick. "The records of employment, as requested."

"Thank you." I took the stick, grateful for the excuse turning and plugging it into the computer provided so my blushing cheeks would not be so evident. "I called you-"

"I never answer while I'm driving."

"Good man." Marco said.

"I try." Nigel shrugged.

"Any luck with your tests?" I asked Nigel. "Do we know what the substance-"

"Not precisely," He said. "But I've at least ruled out some

of the more obvious and most concerning possibilities. My machines are still running; we should know definitively," He checked his watch. "Four hours from now."

"Will there be lasting effects?" Dad asked.

"How can we know that without knowing what it is?" Hailey asked.

"It's not likely." Nigel reassured Dad. "I've spoken with the hospital; Harris is already up and about, and insisting he be released-"

"Will they allow that?" I asked.

Nigel shook his head, smiling to reassure me. "I suspect they'd like to get rid of him, but they're keeping him in overnight as a precaution. He had a far larger dose than either of us, so if he's alright I think we're in the clear."

"I'm glad something's clear." I said. "I feel like I'm going in circles."

"You need more information." Dad said, his answer to just about everything. He was usually right.

"You need to eat." Hailey put in, handing out our food.

"Did you run the names I sent you?" I asked her.

Hailey smiled. "Yes." She pulled up a seat beside me and took over the big screen so we could all see.

"Peebles has his obligatory accounts for work and network interfacing, but only minimal interaction."

I wasn't surprised.

"Dead end?" Marco asked.

"Pretty much." Hailey sighed. "O'Neil wasn't much better. Her posts are erratic, and shallow and flaky when she bothers to make them, but I think that's cause she spends more time out living. She's just not into it."

"McLeod?" I asked.

"Neurotic, possibly obsessive-compulsive activity; likes and leaves a comment - more like a directive - on everyone's posts. She's on-line constantly; I doubt she could get through a meal without documenting and critiquing every second bite. Sad, really."

"Imbalanced?" Dad asked.

"I'd say lonely, unhappy with her lot; this is her chosen escape." Hailey said. "I don't think she's self-aware enough to see it."

"That would fit with the woman I met." I said.

"I would second that." Nigel said. "I've rarely come across anyone so out of step with everyone else."

"Odd ducks..." I said. "Briar told me Paula spends an awful lot of time with Peebles. She thought they were romantically involved, but I didn't see any evidence of that at the Gala."

"Now that you mention it..." Nigel frowned. "They are in frequent proximity, but they're not especially communicative. I suppose that's why I didn't pick up on it; Paula can't seem to stop talking around everyone else."

"Curious." I said. "Finley?" I asked Hailey.

"Finley was tricky," Hailey said. "No chance of a friend request being accepted, but I gleaned through his public stuff; he was very active on a few environmental boards-"

"'Save the whales' type?" Dad asked.

"No - useful ones," Hailey said. "Targeting actual pollution and working to clean it up, and working with industry and government agencies to advise how to prevent it in the first place - stuff that might actually make a difference in people's quality of life. He was one of the good guys." She said sadly as she scrolled through a few of the pages he followed.

"Whoa - stop - back up!" I ordered.

81

She scrolled back. "What's-"

I tapped the screen. "Alderson Holdings..."

Marco's head snapped up. "What you find?"

"I'm not sure." I said. "Maybe nothing. If you don't believe in coincidence-"

"You know what I believe." Marco said, his eyes on the screen.

"Things line up for a reason." Nigel put in, coming over to join us, and bringing the map with him. "Do you have a magnifying glass?"

"Which section?" I asked; he showed me the square with the large cargo vessel, and a blur of color beside it.

I brought the image up on Dad's big screen and zoomed in on the woman with green hair and the man crouched beside her: Briar O'Neil and Dean Finley.

"What are they doing?" Hailey asked.

Nigel tapped the screen, pointing out the vial in Finley's hand. "Taking samples."

"Of what?" Dad asked.

"Algae?" I suggested. "Here." I plugged in my camera card, scrolling through until I found the picture of Dean's microscope slide.

"Back one." Nigel said.

I went back to the picture of Dean's blue-stained fingers. "What is it?"

Nigel drummed his fingers on the back of my chair. "If I had to guess: Omertà."

"As in the code of silence?" Marco asked.

"As in the recently discovered strain of blue-green algae," Nigel explained. "One that leaves a deep blue residue on contact with skin, and emits a rather toxic gas cocktail high in carbon monoxide that causes loss of consciousness before asphyxiating

82

its victims – also known as the silent killer."

"Silent, but violent." Marco chuckled.

Dad chucked him in the back of the head; Marco laughed. "That's the culprit, then."

Nigel frowned. "A lake full of the stuff would be deadly, but a coating on a slide, even a vial full of the stuff? At that concentration you might get a headache."

"We had more than just a headache." I said. "Could it be reacting with something?"

"That's a reasonable hypothesis," Nigel said. "And precisely what I was thinking; we'll know for certain when my tests are complete."

"Where does it come from?" Hailey asked. "Omertà?"

"It's becoming an issue in some South American lakes and shallow, slow-moving rivers." Nigel said. "Canada's northern waters are too cold for it to thrive in any appreciable quantity, and I've never heard of it taking hold in a salt water environment."

"A new strain?" Dad posited.

"I suppose it's a possibility." Nigel looked dubious.

"Is Newell Lake salt water?" Hailey asked.

"It's brackish and cold and very deep." Nigel said. "All qualities that disfavor Omertà developing."

"But here it is." Marco said.

"So it appears." Nigel balled up his empty wrapper and peered out the window, looking in the direction of the lake. "Shall we see for certain?"

"I'm game." I said.

"Car or boat?" Dad asked.

"Boat." Nigel said.

Red Light, Green Light

I slid into the passenger seat of Nigel's car, my stomach fluttering for reasons I didn't want to investigate.

"We weren't thinking." Nigel said as he drove.

"No?" I asked.

"We should have brought the donairs with us."

I laughed.

He grinned. Traffic was light, and Nigel drove fast.

Dad still beat him.

"How, Jake?" Nigel asked.

"Short cut." Dad grinned.

Nigel grabbed vials from his trunk, handing half to me, and half to Marco.

"You keep this stuff with you all the time?" Marco asked.

"Don't judge me." Nigel said, mock affronted.

Marco laughed.

Nigel pulled out a tackle box full of gear. "You never know what you're going to need."

"Truer words..." Dad said, and closed the trunk.

We split up. Dad and Marco boarded the *EquiKnox*, the Knox family trawler; Nigel and I hopped on his cruiser, *Serenity*.

We idled through the marina then sped through the harbor, following the coast line. Cormorant Heights came and went from view, and not much later we turned into the estuary mouth that led to the Newell Sea Link Canal. Its double locks would lift us to Newell Lake. Nigel picked up his radio to hail the lock for service. The first chamber had a green light; we entered the lock slowly.

"Take the bow?" Nigel asked me.

"Gladly." I grabbed the boat hook and moved to the front of the ship, keeping her back from the wall. The lock was quite new, but there were already some good sized pot holes in the concrete wall that could easily catch a fender. I looked back, and saw the *EquiKnox* take position behind us. Nigel dropped a bucket on a rope over the side, hauling up a sample. He dipped in a vial, dried it on his pants and labeled it.

The light turned red as the doors behind us began to close. I sat cross-legged, boat hook in one hand, lock cable in the other, ready to guide us. Water rushed into the chamber, and my stomach sank as the boat rose. Turbulence rocked the boat. I stood, balancing more easily on my feet, shoving hard to keep the fenders from scraping as we ascended. It didn't take long before my head was level with, then passing the top of the lock. The sound of rushing water stilled. The doors in front of us slowly opened. Nigel took another sample. I held the cable line until the light turned green, then dropped it and gave a hard shove off with the boat hook. Nigel idled us ahead into the canal and then picked up speed. Dad and Marco followed in the *EquiKnox*.

I went back to stand beside Nigel.

"You're smiling, Miss Knox."

"I haven't been through here before."

"No? You seemed to know your way around."

"I've had practice. We went through the Great Lakes system when I was 16, then spent over a year at sea."

"That must have been quite the adventure."

"It was." I agreed. "I'd love to go again. I didn't know how much until just now."

"Am I such poor company?" Nigel teased.

I laughed. "Any answer to that might sound incriminating."

He looked straight ahead, watching where we were going. His voice came out low, serious. "There are worse choices."

I didn't know what to say to that. I said nothing.

Nigel pushed the throttle a little more, and radioed ahead to the next lock.

The canal was like a wide and gently curving river, the banks overgrown with flowering blueberry bushes, wild roses, and lupines. We passed under the highway bridges, slowing to take water samples under each. We approached the second, final, and far larger lock. The light was red, but we were in no rush. We pulled to the side, waiting.

The guillotine gate lifted before us, and a gaggle of geese swam alongside us as we entered the lock, waiting placidly for the water to lift them to the lake.

"They seem to have the system down." I said.

"Geese are far more intelligent than most people know." Nigel said.

"Really?"

"They're sure to take over the world."

I laughed, and took over the bow line. The concrete walls rose almost 40 feet around us on all sides. I tilted my head back to look up, and felt infinitesimally small. We took our place alongside the wall, the EquiKnox behind us. Nigel took samples

86

again. This system was a little different; instead of smooth guide ropes, thicker metal cables ran up the walls. I looped our line around the cable, holding it loosely, pressing the boat back from the wall with the hook at the same time.

The door lowered behind us. It felt vaguely ominous as it settled into place, blocking so much of the light. My eyes met Nigel's. Blood rushed into my cheeks and I quickly looked away, feeling nervous and uncomfortable. It was a good thing I wasn't working for Edith; I don't think I would have done a very good job if that was how I was going to react every time he looked at me.

I stayed on my feet this time as the water rose, slurping and sloshing around us. The boat dipped sharply in the turbulence and I dropped to one knee, my right hand burning from the rope tearing across my skin while my left hand pushed hard with the hook to keep us back from the wall. I whimpered and switched hands, bracing the hook awkwardly between my hip and my elbow, blood dripping from my palm.

We crested the wall. The gate ahead of us opened and the red light turned green. I dropped the line, and nearly dropped the hook trying to shove us clear of the wall. I gritted my teeth, braced the pole against my hip and pushed hard. We were away. Nigel brought us ahead through the lock, picking up speed as we crossed the lake. Dad tooted his horn and waved as he and Marco went to the far side of the lake to gather samples there.

I made my way to the console beside Nigel, my arm tucked up gingerly to protect my hand.

Nigel was on the radio, excoriating the lock operator for having the flow rate too high, and slammed the receiver down in fury. "How badly are you hurt?"

"I'll live."

He grabbed my hand to see, hissing at the torn skin. "Take the wheel." He ordered.

I steered with my left hand, keeping my right hand pressed against my chest so the air wouldn't make it sting.

Nigel ducked into the hold, emerging moments later with his tackle box. He pulled out a first aid kit. "Can you keep steady, or should I radio your father-"

"I can manage." I assured him. I kept a death grip on the wheel, refusing to look at the damage on my hand.

The sharp smell of alcohol that filled my nostrils made me lightheaded.

Nigel slid his arm around my waist, holding me up. "Lean against me."

I did as ordered, my back against his chest. My breath came in sharp gasps, dreading what was coming.

Nigel held my wrist firmly. "I'm sorry." He poured the alcohol over my hand.

I shuddered and moaned, but kept our course.

He sprayed something on my torn skin, and the pain stopped.

I slumped in relief against him, breathing deeply. My shoulders relaxed, and the tension in my jaw let go. I flexed my fingers easily. The bleeding had stopped, and some kind of smooth and shiny film sealed off the damaged tissue.

I pushed away from Nigel, smiling sheepishly. "What is that?"

"Something I've been playing with." He said. "I've been waiting for a good test subject."

"I'm happy to be your guinea pig."

He laughed diabolically. "You might change your mind when it wears off."

"How soon will that be?" I asked nervously.

"You're supposed to tell me that." He smiled as he wrapped

my hand in gauze. "I'm hoping several hours at least. If I've gotten it right, you may not notice much of a transition at all."

"Transition?"

"To new skin. The serum is a pain reliever, a styptic, and it encourages hyper-regrowth of tissue. A battlefield medic in a bottle." He took the wheel. "I want my work to heal people, not hurt them."

I took the seat beside him. "How would your work hurt people?"

"Peebles' project idea was a variation on one of my formulas."

"You were so sure it wasn't-"

"I can't help considering it now. I see little signs of any algae so far, let alone Omertà. If it were to grow anywhere, it would have been in the canal. If my formula was what Peebles released into the lab-"

"It wouldn't be your fault."

"It would be my fault for not cutting him off the second I had concerns. Dean Finley would still be alive right now. I wouldn't let myself believe Harris capable of..." He shook his head. I knew Nigel well enough now to know this was his grief talking, and it was guilt weighing him down. "I looked away-"

"You couldn't have known. Not with Harris Peebles. And not with Charlie Bevan." His sharp intake of breath told me I'd hit the mark; the woman who murdered his best friend, and blamed Nigel for it... "That's not how decent people behave." I reminded him. "If he did this, then it was his choice. Not yours."

"I should have acted sooner-"

"You're acting now." I squeezed his hand with my good one. "And you're not acting alone. We'll figure it out. We'll find the truth."

Nigel squeezed back. He pushed the throttle all the way.

Turbulence

We called Dad off the hunt, and met at the docks behind Essex Labs.

"If it's not Omertà," Dad asked as he clambered aboard the Serenity. "What is it?"

Marco pointed to Alderson Holdings.

"Sometimes it's faster to ask." I pulled out my phone and called a man I didn't want to talk to.

"Dover?" My least favorite coroner, Stuart Proust, answered.

"Knox." I corrected. I needed to text the phone company again.

Proust grunted. He didn't want to talk to me either.

"Dean Finley." I said.

He inhaled sharply, preparing to launch into his standard defensive whine. "I'm already running the tox-"

I cut him off. "Have you looked at his fingers?"

"They're blue."

"I noticed." I pinched the bridge of my nose. "Do you know why?"

"Are you going to tell me?"

"I was hoping you could tell me?"

"Keep hoping." He hung up.

I hung my head. "So much for that idea."

Marco continued to point.

I followed the direction of his finger. "That's the same boat-"

"From the map." Nigel finished my sentence.

"Take her away, Cap'n." Dad said.

"Aye, Sir." Nigel pulled away from the dock, and headed for the shipyards.

A huge crane was lifting crates from the back of a truck, looking like some giant devouring insect rather than its namesake, and then loading them onto the ship. Emptied, the truck peeled away and another took its place. I could hear beeping and the sounds of engines and pulleys, but I couldn't hear a single voice giving directions. I stood on tiptoe, and saw not a single human.

"Not jiving." Marco frowned.

"No one to jive." I said. "It's all automated?"

"Every part." Nigel confirmed. "State of the art, overseen remotely. Goods are removed from ship, and placed into storage or directly onto shipping truck. It's very efficient."

"And keeps oh so many people off the government dole." I snarked. I wondered just where all the jobs Edith said she'd created happened to be, because they certainly weren't on the docks.

"I would have to cut my labor force drastically to make up for shipping costs if it were otherwise." Nigel said acidly. "So, yes, indeed it does."

I bit my lip.

My father pursed his mouth, a sure sign he was displeased with me. I wasn't sure I wanted to delve into that. I was sure I'd hear about it later.

"Pull up there." Marco saved the day, pointing again.

Nigel pulled up to the pier and we piled out. I took the bow line almost by rote and secured it to the bollard, frowning at my father when he double checked my line. Old habits... We walked up and around the prow of the ship, coming to the starboard side where we'd seen Briar O'Neil and Dean Finley gathering their sample. I felt dwarfed by the monstrous vessel beside us, and hoped the crane lifting the massive crate overhead was reliable.

"Well," Nigel said, craning his head to take in the side of the ship. "That solves one mystery."

Deep blue spray-paint, the same blue as the streaks on Dean Finley's fingers, adorned the side of the ship: MODERN TECHNOLOGY OWES ECOLOGY AN APOLOGY!

"One of the good guys?" Marco shook his head.

"He'd gone to the dark side." Dad sad sadly.

I rubbed my temples. "He cared deeply."

"His care was misplaced, and ultimately pointless." Nigel said irritably. "Who would even see this?"

Marco reached up to rub the paint; it wiped away. "Water based?"

"The next rain will wash it away." Dad was dumbfounded.

Nigel looked equally flabbergasted. "His statement won't even be lasting! Why would he even bother?"

It was obvious to me. "To try and impress the woman he was with; one that wasn't interested in him."

The men uttered sounds of disgust.

I was glad they were bonding, I guess. "Do you have any more vials?" I asked Nigel.

"Always." He pulled one from his pocket to prove the point. "Why?"

I used it to scrape a sample of the green-brown algae from the side of the ship, and wished I hadn't.

Marco buried his face in his shirt.

"That's vile." Nigel held his nose.

"That's definitely what I smelled coming from the vent." I said. "But I'm not getting the headache or dizziness–"

Dad took the vial from me. "I don't think we need to push it."

"I do think we need to test it." Nigel held out his hand for it. "I need to test it." He corrected. "If I can isolate it from the other samples we'll know what it was that killed Finley that much faster."

Finley, not Dean? He'd lost respect for the man.

"Find the means; figure out who's responsible." Dad nodded.

"Just in time for dinner." Marco added hopefully.

I shook my head at him. "Will you join us for that, Dr. Essex?"

"Thank you, no, Miss Knox." His tone was slightly caustic towards me; he'd lost respect for me... "I have a date."

"Oh." Well, there goes my heart. "Some other time."

Nigel dropped us off at the EquiKnox, and took the vial full of the vile algae inside. My hand started to sting as we entered the first lock. There was less turbulence as we descended, or maybe I just noticed it less. My hand throbbed as we left the second lock and headed into the bay. I didn't care. My heart hurt so much more.

Paula-tics

W e made it back to the office in one piece, and I got back to deflecting. Hard. I checked over the records of employment, and learned next to nothing new about any of our persons of interest. I called Paula McLeod and tried Briar O'Neil again; neither one answered. I called the hospital; visiting hours weren't for another hour. I needed to clear my head before I dealt with Peebles anyway. I drove toward my kayak, and had just pulled into the marina parking lot when my phone rang.

Paula McLeod had the worst timing.

It felt deliberate.

She did agree to meet, though. I looked with longing at the marina, the sparkling blue water beckoning to me, then turned around and drove back to her apartment complex. It was a new build, rather cookie-cutter, and nothing like the complex Briar lived in. HR must not have ranked as well as scientists in the pay department.

Paula frowned when she opened the door. "I never wear green next to my hair like that; I always thought it made me look like a Christmas tree." She flounced her navy blue skirt set, emphasizing the comparison. "I see from your example that I made the right choice."

I brushed self-consciously at the front of my cardigan.

"Do come in." She waved me in with a gracious gesture.

I narrowly refrained from elbowing her in the midsection when passing.

I felt like I'd stepped into a dollhouse. Everything was spic and span and symmetrical, and covered in florals and laces and and ruffles. The settee I was directed to had to have been antique, and stuffed with its original horse hair. It made a crunching sound reminiscent of steel wool being compressed as I sat on it, and felt about as comfortable. The antimacassar behind my head kept flopping onto my head, but I was loathe to move it as its twin behind Paula's head stayed in perfect order. I wasn't sure how it managed to stay in place with all her head wagging and jaw gaping. Maybe it was afraid of her? Or maybe it didn't want to be lectured?

She was lecturing me now, giving me an unrequested primer on the proper complimentary colors I should choose to compliment my particular shade of scarlet hair.

I regretted my earlier restraint.

"I assume you are here about the incident at the lab today?" She scraped her spoon against the sides of her tea cup as she stirred, producing a sound like nails on a chalkboard.

I cringed, and set my cup on the coffee table before me. "The incident?"

"Dean Finley." She tsked. "I heard all about it on the news. He was rather erratic," She leaned forward conspiratorially, cupping her hand beside her mouth. "ADD." She whispered as if it were some horrid clandestine secret that might be overheard; who was supposed to overhear it in her living room I couldn't guess. "I am surprised something had not happened to him sooner."

"You don't seem upset."

"It is tragic, I suppose, but we were not close. He should have been more careful."

"You believe it was an accident?"

"What else could it be?" She wrinkled her nose distastefully. "It was careless negligence, is what it was. Harry might have been seriously injured. Now that would have been a tragic loss."

"You and Mr. Peebles-"

"Dr. Peebles." She corrected instantly. "We are very close." That made confirmation from three sources; Briar, Nigel, and now Paula herself.

I still had trouble believing it. "Forgive me, but last night at the Spring Gala, you did not seem to be close at all. I didn't see you exchange even a single word."

"To an obtuse outside observer perhaps we might not seem close, but I assure you, we are."

I had to bite my cheek to hold in the retort I wanted to make.

"Harry and I are so in tune with one another, we hardly need to exchange a word to understand what the other is thinking. We spent the whole afternoon that way, I in my seat, and he beside me in his hospital bed, our gazes locked upon one another, communing on a higher plane."

"A higher plane?"

"That is what Harry calls it. We can sit silently in one another's presence and be content. It is our normal."

"Is it normal for Dr. Peebles to go in to work on the weekend?"

"I suppose."

"You suppose?" I asked. "You are very close; shouldn't you know?"

"What does it matter when he comes and goes, as long as he comes back?" She tilted her head, examining me like an insect she couldn't name but definitely didn't want in her living room. "I am not desperate and clingy like some women, constantly keeping tabs, chasing after a man so high out of her league she must have vertigo looking up at him." She looked down her nose at me.

I gritted my teeth and balled my fists, fighting hard an urge to head-butt her nose. "Vertigo?" I tilted my head. Where had I heard that term, almost that exact expression...

"You seem to be a little tense." Paula noted. "Perhaps your blood sugar–"

"My blood sugar is just fine." I snapped. "My rising blood pressure is far more concerning–"

"There are pills for that." She smiled sweetly and blinked innocently, reaching out awkwardly to tap my knee.

A thought hit me like a cast-iron skillet: was she actually sincere?

I reconsidered everything she'd said to me, and the way that she'd said it. It wasn't arrogance; she honestly believed she was being helpful.

I looked around the room with new eyes. Now that I knew what to look for, it was obvious. Ordered, efficient, symmetrical. A doll house. If she were a little boy, it might have been a train collection, or toy cars lined up against the wall. The beyond awkward social miscues, the blunt and tactless suggestions, the obsessive need to follow rules: Autism.

I looked at the woman with new eyes, and wanted to weep. What a horrible fit this job was for her; a diversity hire plugged in for the sake of some quota, but not for her sake or the sake of the people she would have to interact with. It made me furious.

97

She was trying so hard, doing her best, but she just didn't see, and no one had bothered to tell her. Not in a way she could grasp. I tried. "Paula, I don't think Harris Peebles is your friend."

"But he is nice to me."

"In what way?"

"He listens to me. He is patient. He never argues or yells. He lets me tell him everything."

My alarm bells clanged. "What do you tell him? What does he ask you about?"

She smiled. "What everyone is working on."

"What was Dean Finley working on?"

"That is confidential."

"But you could tell Harris?"

"Of course. He is my co-worker; we are allowed to talk in house."

"Is that an official rule, or what he told you?"

She sat up straighter, thinking rapidly, her face draining of color. "He told me..." Her voice tapered off. She started to rock, swaying slowly back and forth, soothing herself.

My heart broke; I knew I'd just broken hers. "Did you do any work for him?" I asked. "Anything on the computer system?"

"Not for Dr. Peebles." She shook her head slowly; I noticed the name change; he wasn't Harry to her anymore. She was distancing herself from him. Good.

"For someone else?"

"Briar O'Neil." She grimaced.

My heart pounded. My head spun. Vertigo... "What did she have you do?"

"I opened and sent some files using Dr. Peebles' computer when hers was occupied."

"Who did you send them to?"

She wrote down a list for me, a series of generic numbered e-mail addresses that I never could have remembered.

"Did Dr. Peebles know?" I asked.

She tilted her head, considering. I waited for her to process. "I think he did."

I compressed my lips.

"Did I do something very wrong?" She looked very concerned, wringing her fingers as well as rocking now, little tics that showed her upset.

"Not intentionally." I said; she still looked worried. "No." I said; she relaxed considerably. "But I think Briar did."

"I do not think that she is my friend either."

"No, Paula." I said sadly. "I don't think she is."

Peebles

I sped up the road to Briar O'Neil's; she wasn't home, and she wasn't answering her phone. I left another message, then drove east to the hospital, paid for parking, and got Harris Peebles' room number from the information kiosk. It bothered me that I could do that so easily; no ID, no checks of any kind. Same thing at the ward nurses station; I just smiled and was waved on through; they were too busy to care if I belonged or not.

The hospital reminded me of the police station; frenetically busy, constantly in flux, noise level just below a roar. It wasn't a restful atmosphere by any stretch of the imagination. It wasn't a place I wanted to be.

From the pinched look on his face when I entered his room, it wasn't a place Harris Peebles wanted to be either.

"Dr. Peebles?" I smiled. "How are you feeling?"

He didn't try to hide his sneer this time, hostile from the get-go.

I didn't believe for a second that this man was or ever had been suicidal, but my gut and the alarm bells ringing in my head were telling me he was dangerous.

"Miss Knot."

That was on purpose. Meant to annoy me?

"Knox." I corrected, maintaining my smile.

It seemed to annoy him. Sometimes that backfired, but sometimes that worked in your favor; my gut said it might be the best way to make him talk. I noticed a pair of sunglasses on the bedside table: sky blue, a woman's style, and most definitely not his; most likely Paula's.

"Have you had any visitors today?" I already knew the answer to that, but his response could give me a baseline to gauge him.

"I hardly see how that's any of your business." He narrowed his eyes. The cringing man from last night wasn't evident; this was his Nigel suit talking, and he sounded defensive. That made me curious.

"Dr. Essex has made it my business." Blunt for blunt. My Nigel appreciated straightforwardness; I hoped this false image did as well. My Nigel? Good grief, Bethany. I felt ridiculous.

Peebles picked up on it. He leered, openly dismissive of me. "If Dr. Essex wishes to know, he can speak to me himself."

"Dr. Essex chose to delegate." I said coolly, taking a page from Edith. "He has more important tasks to attend to."

Peebles balked at that. He curled his fingers, wincing, revealing a crack in his Nigel-plated armor. He darted his eyes away from me.

I'd knocked him off guard. I pressed hard. "Have you had any other visitors today, Mr. Peebles?"

"One." He replied begrudgingly.

"Who?"

"Miss McLeod left not long ago."

No wonder he was hostile; I wondered just how far to press him now. I eased back. "Have you had any lingering effects from this morning?"

"None."

I pressed. "Were you aware that Dean Finley died?"

"I am aware." His tongue darted out like a lizard's, licking his lips.

That gave me the creeps. He knew. He just didn't care at all, he may even have been pleased. Had he killed him? That thought disturbed me. I tried not to let it show. I eased back. "Have you any idea what it was we breathed in?" I asked. "Dr. Essex wasn't able to determine-"

He smiled at that, but not cringing; it was that smug expression, more Nigel-than-Nigel, a caricature of him. "He's not as smart as he thinks he is."

"He seems to be getting by." I said dryly. "He has everything a man could want-"

"Not everything." He sneered.

"What is he missing?" I tilted my head, trying to get a handle on him. "Is he as smart as you?"

"Oh, I sincerely doubt that-" He cut himself off sharply, glaring at me; he'd let out more than he'd meant.

I smiled, and then I switched tactics, trying to get him to let out more. "Dr. Essex remarked on that to me."

"Oh?"

"He said you were the most brilliant man he'd ever met, and feels grateful to have your skills and talents on his team-"

"His team?" Peebles swallowed convulsively. Head nodding became head shaking, refusing to hear what I'd told him. His eyes bulged with fury, his hands clenched, choking his wrists, his nails dug in. His top lip disappeared, swallowed up in seething rage.

Why? Over what? That wasn't the reaction I'd anticipated; I'd miscalculated here. I'd misjudged something horribly.

I ran with it. "You are the lynch pin in his operations, without you it all falls apart. He said he couldn't do without you."

"He would never say something like that!" Peebles seethed. "He would never be so weak!"

"That was exactly what he told me. His precise words, in fact."

"You're lying."

"To what end?" I asked him. "What would I gain by lying?"

"Women enjoy lying."

"Some more than others." I was careful not to disagree; I didn't want him to shut down. He was right on the edge of it. "What woman lied to you? Paula McLeod?"

He sneered; strike one.

"Briar O'Neil?"

He cringed; home run.

"What did she lie about?"

"What do you gain by knowing?"

"It's always good to know the truth."

"Well, you're the investigator. I'm sure you can figure it out."

My heart started to pound. "I'm sure you could give me a hint."

"I could."

"What am I missing?"

"The point."

"What is the point, Mr. Peebles?"

His smile didn't reach his eyes. "I think we're done now, Miss Knot. You know the way out."

I stood to leave, feeling flustered and afraid. What did he mean? What was I supposed to figure out? How long did I have to find out? I had a foreboding sense that time was not on my side. My eyes fell on the baby blue glasses on the table beside him.

Paula wore navy. They weren't hers. That would be against the rules.

I turned to meet his eyes. "Briar was here."

"What of it?" His eyes narrowed. Hostile again. He didn't like that I knew.

"Women aren't the only ones that like to lie."

He cringed at my tone.

"What work was she doing on your computer?"

His tongue darted out, his eyes bulged. Why?

"What are you hiding, Mr. Peebles?"

"Doctor–"

"Dr. Essex sent me to find the truth."

"You couldn't find the truth if–"

"You could tell me." I said. "Or don't you trust your boss to know?" I probed. "Don't you trust yourself?"

"You don't know anything!" He was close to breaking.

I pushed him over the edge. "I know where you keep your vision board. I know who you want to become."

I hated myself. I hated what I was doing to him. Anything for the truth? I'd just violated any hope of trust; I'd become that thing on the board, that side he feared and hated. I was no better than Edith. I was worse. I was Jeff.

"What am I missing?" I demanded. "What is the point, Mr. Peebles?"

"I'm sure it will become apparent soon enough." He smiled, the cringing man gone, utterly destroyed, consumed by his version of Nigel.

I'd pushed him too far.

"Everyone will see."

I felt real fear then. "What are you planning?"

"Stop looking." Dad said; I compressed my lips. "A watched pot never boils. Focus on something else; trust your brain to make the connections."

I rubbed the sore spot on my head. "I can't make the connections if I don't-"

"Step back from it." He kissed my forehead. "Trust yourself."

"I don't trust him."

"Who?"

"Peebles. He's planning something. He may have already done it-"

"I'll talk to Patience." Dad pulled out his phone.

I tried Nigel again, then Briar, then Marco, then gave in. I needed to move. What bothered me most... "I'll call you later."

"Where are you going?" Dad asked.

"Essex Labs."

"Bethany, wait-"

I ran out the door and into my van. I headed for the highway, and got stuck in traffic. A line stretched ahead as far as I could see, and was beginning to pile up behind me as well. I flipped on my police scanner; there was a massive accident on the highway ahead, blocking both lanes. It would be hours before it was clear. I swung a u-turn in the middle of the road, and was honked at. I backtracked, then followed down the Cove roads, headed for the marina.

I called Dad. "Can you meet me at the marina?"

"The road's blocked solid; it'll be awhile before I can get out."

"Can I take the Knox?"

"You can't manage the canals alone in that-"

"The other one."

"Be careful, Beth."

"I always am." I hung up.

107

I tried Nigel again; no answer. I held the phone in my hand, debating, shaking. I could manage the boat on my own, but I sure didn't want to. I dialed.

"Beth?" Sam whispered incredulously, trying to hide that he was speaking with me.

"I need help."

"I can't-"

"Please! It's life and death - there's no one else-"

"I can't. Don't ever call me again." He hung up.

I parked and climbed into the back of the van, my breath coming in hitched sobs as I dug through my junk door for the spare keys. I ripped the drawer out and dumped it upside down on the floor. Found them. I grabbed them and ran for the dock. The Serenity was gone from its slip. The EquiKnox loomed up before me. I passed it, and pulled the cover off the Hard Knox, Dad's ancient speedboat, mostly driven by my brother now. I untied the lines, hurling them aboard, and jumped in. The keys slid into the ignition. I turned them. The engine clanked, sputtered, knocked, and died.

"Johnny!" I cursed my brother. "Why can't you take care of this thing!"

I tried again. And again. The third time it caught. The engine roared to life. I peeled out of the slip and into the bay. I flew past Cormorant Heights. I looked over at Nigel's dock as I went by; no boat, and no lights on in his house either. That was good. In my present mood if he had been there not answering his phone he wouldn't have had to worry about Peebles or anything else ever again.

I turned into the estuary and radioed the lock for service. The light was red. I cut roughly to the side, third in line, waiting impatiently for it to change, my heart pounding with adrenaline, fueled by fear. What had he done? I tried Nigel again, desperately, willing him to answer. He didn't.

The lock doors opened. A cruiser I didn't recognize idled out, followed closely by the Serenity.

"Nigel!" His name tore out from me.

Every head on every ship turned to look at me.

I wanted the water to swallow me under.

It didn't.

"Miss Knox?" Nigel veered his ship towards me.

I nearly wept with relief. "Peebles-"

"Cris, take over." Nigel directed one of his guests on board to take the wheel. "Take her home. I'll join you when I can."

"This is a shoddy deal," Cris complained. "We can't go without our host!"

"You're abandoning me?" Celia Vanderly pouted, her lower lip protruding in disbelief.

"Can't be helped, darling." Nigel leaned to kiss her cheek.

She turned her face so her mouth met his, slid her fingers into his hair and pulled him in tighter.

My heart shattered. I looked away.

Someone whistled and catcalled.

"I'll call you later." Nigel told her breathlessly when she released him.

I nearly threw up.

"You'd better." She proclaimed victoriously.

He stepped aboard the Hard Knox, rocking it as he did. The Serenity carried on without him.

"These are for you." He set down my clipboard and my bag.

"My laptop?"

"The police allowed me to take them when they left."

"Thank you."

"What's happened?" Nigel demanded.

"I'm worried." I said. "I saw Peebles in the hospital–"

"And?" Nigel pressed.

"He made ominous statements; planning to show everyone. He wouldn't say what he was planning–"

"That would be asking too much." Nigel frowned.

"I think he's already done it. I needed to..." I struggled with what to say, gesturing weakly ahead.

He took the wheel. "Yes." He agreed, understanding at once what I couldn't put into words.

I slumped in relief as the boat moved ahead into the lock, then stopped again, waiting again. "I also spoke with Paula McLeod; Briar O'Neil had her open and send files to these addresses using Peebles' computer." I handed him the slip of paper Paula had given to me.

His frown deepened as he scanned them. "These mean nothing to me." He handed it back.

That didn't surprise me. "I'd hoped you'd know." I said, and moved up to secure the bow line.

Water filled the chamber, the sound drowning out any words we might have said. The boat dipped and bucked in the turbulence. I dreaded the next chamber.

We filed out in an orderly row behind the other ships; Nigel passed them as soon as he was able.

"This thing has some kick." Nigel patted the console appreciatively.

"As long as she doesn't give out." I frowned. "My brother's not the most diligent about her maintenance."

"Pity." Nigel said. "What does he do?"

"He's a mechanic."

He laughed, and pushed the throttle a little more, but slowed almost immediately. Everyone and their dog was out for a Saturday evening cruise, filling both sides of the canal, talking genially with their neighbors across the water. Nigel zipped alongside, skirted around, or darted between them, wherever there was room.

"Oi! Watch your wake!" A man yelled and his dog barked at us as we passed.

I hardly noticed for the questions filling my head, and the fear squeezing my heart. "What's the connection..."

"Between?" Nigel asked.

I didn't realize I'd spoken out loud. "Briar O'Neil and Peebles." I said. "He said she'd lied to him. What about?"

Nigel pursed his lips. "I don't know. I rarely saw them together, certainly not since Paula..."

"Before Paula?" I asked. My heart contracted. I knew from his expression before he said it.

"They were together." He turned to granite. "Harris wasn't the only one that changed. Briar left him for Dean."

"Briar has red hair." It should have been obvious.

I thought back to that first night, the Spring Gala; her caustic attack on Paula, then the way she had avoided looking at Peebles, and Peebles had avoided looking at her; she was jealous, and so was he. The tension was there. I hadn't seen it. I hadn't looked for it. "Peebles was targeting Dean in revenge."

"He must have been." Nigel smacked the wheel. "Dean was a test sample. Blast it - I should have seen! I was so focused on Peebles as the thief-"

"We both were." I shook my head. "Hell hath no fury like a woman scorned... I guess that applies to men, too."

"But what becomes of a man scorned?" Nigel asked.

"Who does he become?" I asked. "Someone else." I answered

111

myself, at least in Peebles' case. "Test sample? What was his project?" I asked, afraid to ask, afraid of the answer. "The one you turned down?"

"Chemical warfare."

"Everyone will see... He's targeting everyone?"

Nigel pushed the throttle. He radioed ahead to the next lock.

I texted Patience. She texted right back. "Darn it. Peebles let himself out of the hospital–"

"When?"

"Almost an hour ago." I hoped he was stuck on the highway somewhere behind that accident; I texted Dad.

Marco texted me back; he was with Dad, they were on their way in the EquiKnox. I pulled out my laptop, and entered the security codes he gave me that let me into the Alderson Holdings' surveillance system. I accessed the cameras overlooking the entrance to Essex Labs and tilted the screen so Nigel could see. "Do you know what Peebles drives?"

"The silver Jag." He tapped the car on the screen.

I scrolled back through the footage, watching the time stamp. "He's only just arrived." I let Chief Patience know.

We approached the second, final, and far larger lock. The light was red.

"Blast it!" Nigel let out a string of expletives, and pulled to the side, waiting helplessly.

The guillotine gate lifted before us; it seemed to take forever. The massive boat inside left the chamber at the slowest possible rate it could manage, so slow it was passed on its way out by a mother duck and her brood. Nigel ground his teeth. An eternity passed before the light turned green. The Hard Knox surged ahead, only to pull over and stop again.

I took the bow line by rote, keeping a death grip on the boat hook with my left hand, and a nervous one on the line with my right. There was no pain, no stinging, but I hadn't looked under the gauze to check my skin. The gauze would be flimsy protection if the rope lurched again. The guillotine dropped, sealing us inside the chamber.

Water dribbled in; the flow rate had been lowered. My heart swelled with relief, but my jaw tightened with tension. It reduced the turbulence, but it meant the chamber filled slowly. I held the line, willing the procedure to go faster. It was taking too long, going too slow, never ending. I looked back to see Nigel looking at me; I couldn't look away this time. I held his gaze as I held the cable line and we rose.

We finally crested the wall. Another eternity passed before the gate ahead of us opened and the red light turned green. I dropped the line, gritted my teeth, and then pushed away.

Nigel brought us ahead as fast as he dared through the lock, then picked up speed as fast as he could to cross the lake. A plume of water sprayed behind us as we skipped over the water, trying to catch up to Harris Peebles, trying to stop whatever he had planned.

Vertigo

We pulled up to the docks behind Essex Labs. I got on my hands and knees and pried off the panel under the console. I rolled onto my back, running my fingers along the ledge until I found what I was looking for: Dad's pistol. I unwrapped it from its oil-cloth wrappings and checked the chamber; 6 rounds. Nigel cut the engine as I leaped to the pier, securing the bow line. I ran for the door while he tied aft. I dug in my bag as I ran, pulling out my cloner; I swiped the entry pad and the door opened. Nigel sprinted up the steps two at a time; I held the door for him, then followed him up the stairs to the third floor. I could smell the fumes in the stairwell, the sickening green-brown algae smell mixed with whatever concoction had turned it deadly, growing stronger the higher we went.

"It's worse." I coughed.

"I noticed." Nigel snapped. "Hold your breath as long as you can."

I took in a deep breath and kept chasing him up the stairs.

He swiped the door open at the fourth floor, and took a breath. "It's clear."

114

I gasped like an asthmatic fish, my lungs burning, my heart pounding. I could still smell the algae, but nowhere near as strong.

"Down here." He led me to the end of the hall, swiping an entry pad and entering a code to open a secure door.

"What is this?"

"Clean room." He passed me a gas mask and blue hazmat suit.

"Security cameras in the halls?" I asked. "I'd like to see what we're walking into."

Nigel turned on a console and entered his codes into the system. The screens showed nothing but static. "Blast it! I'm locked out."

"May I?" I leaned over him, and tried the few tricks I knew. I wasn't Hailey; they weren't enough to get through. "Darn it. If you ever need any locks opened..."

"I know who to call for that." He tapped my helmet.

I pulled the gear on over my clothes and Nigel taped the seams; I did the same for him. The gas mask was uncomfortable, the air tanks heavy; more like a scuba system than the face filters we wore earlier. Sweat trickled between my shoulder blades and I itched like crazy under the thick blue suit, but I was glad of it as we descended the stairs to the third floor.

The glass panel on the stairwell door was flecked with an unhealthy looking greenish-brown residue. Nigel looked at me. I could tell he was debating whether or not to let me enter.

"Let's go." I said, not allowing him the option.

I was holding a gun; he didn't argue.

Nigel put his hand to the door and stopped as a powerful humming sounded.

"What is that?" I asked.

"The air filters turned on." He pushed open the door.

The brown flecks in the air swirled and spun and began to disappear, sucked into the powerful vents above our head.

"In the halls too?" I asked. "Not just the labs?"

"The whole floor, in case of breach. Each floor has its own separate system."

The system was working perfectly now. The flecks that had settled on the walls and the floor peeled off and joined the dance, whisking and winding their way into the vents; it looked like muddy rain falling up. I was glad to see it go.

"Where is it controlled?" I asked.

"This way." Nigel led me down a corridor and around a bend, stopping in front of a metal door. "Blast it! Not again!" His fob didn't work.

"This part–" I reached for my bag, and remembered I'd left it upstairs when I'd put on the hazmat suit.

Turns out I didn't need it. The handle turned and the door pulled open.

I raised my pistol.

Briar O'Neil tried to slam the door shut, but Nigel put his foot in the gap.

I lowered my gun so I wouldn't hit him.

"Miss O'Neil." Nigel said. "Care to explain?"

She backed away, shaking her head, then her whole body shaking as she sobbed. "I didn't mean to…"

"Didn't mean what?" Nigel demanded angrily.

She cringed.

I put my hand on his arm and shook my head; he stepped back out of the way. I held the gun behind my back, out of Briar's sight, and peeled off my mask and hood; I didn't need it anymore.

"You didn't mean to hurt Dean?" I guessed; she nodded her head and peeled off her mask, taking a layer of weight off with it. I bowed my head, keeping my voice soft and soothing. "What happened, Briar? I know you were at Alderson Holdings after the Gala." Her shoulders slumped; she was ready to talk. "Dean spray painted the ship-"

Her head lifted, correcting a detail. "A filthy ship carrying filthy-"

"A ship carrying raw supplies to make our clean solar film!" Nigel broke in; I could have smacked him. "One that was going to help the environment and thousands of people-" He finally caught on to my motioning and bit his tongue.

Briar was sobbing again, too upset to speak now. I linked my arm through hers and led her from the room, hoping a change in scene would bring a change in her emotions. I took her up the hall to the lounge beside the elevators, giving her time to calm down and get hold of herself. She curled up in the corner of a couch, a bit more secure, a bit more safe. I sat down across from her, keeping my feet on the floor, my body turned slightly towards her; non-threatening, actively listening. Nigel had the sense to stay out of view, hovering around the corner where he could hear, and I could see him, but Briar could not.

I decided to overlook the spray paint aspect; I took a different line altogether. "You had Paula run numbers for you, on Harris Peebles' computer."

She tilted her head, confused. "System tests."

That kind of tester. Darn it. "The e-mails you sent the data to?"

"Mine." She said. "Company, if you want to be technical."

"I do. I need to." I said. I needed her to be as well. "Dean took a sample of something from the ship; a rather pungent something."

She smiled fondly. "It was very pungent."

"And Dean liked to play jokes..."

"That's all it was supposed to be. We sealed up Harry's office and put the algae in the vent to bug him."

"You'd have to live with it, too, in your lab next door."

"Dean said it was a small price to pay." She gave a sobbing laugh. "He paid too much. He paid way too much."

"And you knocked out the security tapes to hide it?"

She nodded.

"And what else?" I had a fair idea.

"I reversed the vent fan so it would blow out." She cried; Nigel held his head in his hands and slumped to the floor, his back against the wall. "Whatever was in it must have mixed with – I didn't mean to hurt him." She started to sob hysterically. "I didn't mean–"

"I believe you, Briar. I know it was an accident, but–"

"I fixed it." She said desperately, trying to assuage her guilt. "I had to purge the system, but I put it back."

"But it won't put Dean back."

"It won't hurt anyone else." She said.

My head snapped up. I surged to my feet and ran, my heart pounding, the world tilting as a crazy spinning vertigo took hold of me. I rounded the corner and turned. Peebles door was locked. I banged on it, standing on my toes to look through the window. I didn't have my gear; I used what I had. I shot the lock and shoved the door open, sinking to my knees beside Harris Peebles' lifeless body. His flimsy mask hadn't been enough protection.

If I hadn't pushed him...

"Oh my word." Nigel breathed out raggedly, stepping past

me and Peebles to the lab desk.

"What is it?" I asked. I didn't care. I heard noise in the hall; raised voices, running footsteps.

"Beth!"

"Daddy."

My father pushed into the room followed by Marco, and Briar, and Spider, and Jeff. "I heard a gun - oh, dear God." He saw Harris on the floor and shivered.

Briar saw Harris on the floor and fainted. That was probably a blessing.

"Marco, take her out of here." Nigel directed; Marco picked up Briar and carried her out.

"Don't touch anything." Jeff ordered us, trying to assert control. He reached down to help me to my feet.

I gave him a flat look, rising by myself. "I know the drill." I stood beside my father; Jeff narrowed his eyes at me, then he glared at Nigel.

"What is all this?" Spider demanded, reaching for a flask on the lab desk.

"Don't touch it." Nigel snapped; Spider pulled back. "Don't even breathe on it."

"Did he-"

Nigel cut me off. "Briar saved us all." He shifted the flask Spider had been reaching for farther away from the contraption on the desk and capped it tightly. "This acid would have eaten right through our suits, and then us. If Peebles had completed this..." He didn't bother to finish his sentence, staring with dismay at the contraption on the table before him.

"Some kind of bomb?" Spider swallowed nervously.

"A rapid dispersal unit." Nigel said. "The air filters wouldn't have been able to compensate. It might as well be a bomb."

"The gun?" Jeff demanded, holding his hand out to me.

I gritted my teeth, and handed it over.

Jeff shook his head. "Jake, I warned you to get rid of this thing."

"It came in handy." I said.

"It's more trouble than it's worth." Jeff argued. He stood before the smashed out window, reared back to throw it, brought his arm forward, and didn't let go.

Spider grinned, then held his hand above his eyes, peering off into the distance. "It's gone now."

Jeff held the gun out to Dad. "Never to be seen again."

Dad pursed his mouth, then nodded, taking his pistol back.

Jeff went into the hall, closed the door, and fired through the lock. "Dig that out." He told Spider. He smiled at me. "I told you I'd take care of you, baby."

I wrapped my arms around my middle, digging my nails into my elbows. I owed him now. Bile rose in my throat. The room spun. Vertigo...

Justified

I went to Patience's office first thing in the morning with my report. And Dad's gun.

"Sit." She ordered. I sat as she read. She came to the end, laid the report on her desk, and rubbed her temples. "This is a little different from what I was handed earlier."

"Spider's always been a bit... flexible with the truth."

"That's an understatement." She laughed bitterly. Then she picked up my report, tamped the pages neatly, and filed it through the shredder.

"Chief?" I swallowed convulsively, struggling to breathe. "That's clearly manslaughter–"

"Manslaughter?" She shook her head. "Dean Finley's death was an accident, and Briar O'Neil is going to live with that guilt the rest of her life; I think that's enough punishment. As for Harris Peebles... That girl deserves a medal for what she stopped."

"But–"

She held up her hand to cut me off. "Drug dealers and rapists walk free, and my budget keeps shrinking. I'm not going to spend the few men I have left clogging up the system for what amounts to an unfortunate tragedy."

"Spider gets his way."

Patience frowned at me.

"Keeping him on has nothing to do with the union-"

"Spider has his uses." She said evenly. "He always did."

I compressed my lips and nodded, feeling sick inside. She pushed the gun back towards me. That didn't help matters.

"Keep in touch." Patience bent her head over her work, dismissing me. I stogged the gun in my purse, and opened the door to leave. "You still owe me."

I walked away from the station with a thousand pounds of weight on my shoulders.

It didn't lessen as I drove towards Cormorant Heights. I went through the security checkpoint, and turned left onto Cormorant Point Road, following it all the way to the end. Cars lined both sides of Nigel's driveway, his weekly marketing meeting and planning session underway inside. I rang the bell.

The elderly man that answered smiled at me this time, recognizing me from before. "This way, please, Miss."

I smiled. I far preferred that to Madam. I was shown into Nigel's office and left waiting for him. I made my way to the window, watching the boats sail on the sparkling blue ocean, longing to be out on the water. After this...

"Miss Knox." Nigel went straight to his seat behind his desk, establishing that barrier between us straight away.

I wanted to weep. "Dr. Essex." I took the seat across from him as directed.

"For services rendered." He opened a ledger, and slid a cheque across the desktop to me.

I picked it up, goggling at the amount. "But this is three times what we agreed upon."

"I hired you to find a thief, then Dean Finley's killer, and then the truth about Harris Peebles... It was well earned."

I bowed my head, waves of guilt washing over me. "You read my report?"

"And you delivered it." He said stiffly, that solid granite voice. "How was it received by our venerable police chief?"

"Not very well." I admitted. "She ran it through her shred-der."

Nigel threw back his head and laughed as a thousand pounds of weight lifted off his shoulders.

I smiled to see it, feeling not quite so awful as I had.

"Sensible woman." He said.

"Eminently practical." I agreed.

"You're still bothered." He frowned at me.

"It doesn't sit right."

"How could it?" He moved to sit beside me, and took my hand in his. "Nothing about this situation was right. But I believe her decision is justified-"

"It avoids justice-"

"It avoids condemning further a woman who will spend the rest of her life condemning herself. Sometimes we need to be flexible with the rules; this is one of those times. A public shaming in the courts would only add to Briar's misery. It will do nothing to help her. It will not bring back Dean. Frankly, I don't want to think about Harris."

"How will you do without him?" I asked. "You said he was the lynch pin..."

"I am the lynch pin." Nigel shook his head at himself. "That sounds incredibly arrogant, nevertheless, it is true. They are my formulas, and this is still my company, and I will take care... " He picked up my hand, examining the still pink skin on my palm. "This has healed nicely."

My eyes started to leak. I pulled my hand from his, brushing at them, deflecting. "What happens to Briar?"

"A very great deal of counseling." He smiled sadly. "Fortunately, her employer will ensure that she receives whatever she needs."

"Do you think she'll be OK?"

He pursed his lips, thinking, then nodded. "Come with me."

I followed him from the office, down the hall, and stopped at the top of the stairs leading down into the living room. We could see, but not easily be seen. The house was full, people talking and laughing softly; they all knew what had happened, and what had narrowly been avoided. The adults did. Their children darted about happily - inside to their parents, then back outside to the pool or the yard to play - blissfully oblivious. Briar O'Neil sat on the pool's edge, her feet dangling in the water, talking with Paula McLeod. Paula listened attentively, and patted Briar's hand. Awkwardly. Briar smiled.

"I think she'll be OK." Nigel said. He slipped his fingers over mine, and squeezed.

I squeezed back, feeling lighter, feeling free.

The End

«<»>

About the Author

Canadian author Stephanie Turner belongs to the Triple 'E' Club - an Easterner in Economic Exile. She lives with her husband and children in view of the Rocky Mountains, but longs for the shores of the Atlantic Ocean.

Until she can get home, she'll set her stories where her heart is, with occasional treks to drier regions, and the odd quest to galaxies far, far away.

When she's not writing, she can be found wandering through the local bird sanctuary, sketchbook in hand, or curled up in a comfy chair with a good book and a hot cup of tea.

Also by Stephanie Turner

Books in the Bethany Knox Private Investigator Series

Opportunity Knox

Bethany Knox Private Investigator #1

Billionaire scientist Nigel Essex is arrogant, obnoxious, and drop-dead gorgeous. But is he a murderer?

When Nigel Essex is accused of murdering his best friend, Bethany Knox of Opportunity Knox Private Investigators is hired to clear his name.

The trouble is, the jerk nearly ran over her with his boat - twice! - and she's pretty sure he's guilty.

If she doesn't get this right, an innocent man will go to jail, and a murderer will get off Scot-free.

How is she supposed to get past her first impression to find the truth?

Conductor of Crime

Bethany Knox Private Investigator #2

Nigel was positively enjoying himself. "Are you saying I inadvertently brokered a deal with a crime boss?"

Darn it. I could have kicked him for not taking this seriously.

When Nigel Essex needs help recovering his stolen sports car, Bethany Knox of Opportunity Knox Private Investigators is hired to find it.

But when the thief turns out to be the nephew of a local crime boss, will she end up finding more than she bargained for?

Manufactured by Amazon.ca
Bolton, ON